TRUE HEROES

TRUE HEROES

A TREASURY OF MODERN-DAY FAIRY TALES
WRITTEN BY BEST-SELLING AUTHORS

PHOTOGRAPHY BY JONATHAN DIAZ

SHADOW
MOUNTAIN

Visit us at ShadowMountain.com

Library of Congress Cataloging-in-Publication Data

True heroes : a treasury of modern-day fairy tales written by best-selling authors / edited by Jonathan Diaz ; with Shannon Hale, Brandon Mull, Ally Condie, Jennifer A. Nielsen ; photographs by Jonathan Diaz.

    pages cm

  Summary: Twenty-one bestselling authors have written short stories to accompany Jonathan Diaz's fantastical photographs of children who are battling cancer.

    ISBN 978–1–62972–103–3 (hardbound : alk. paper) 1. Children's stories. 2. Adventure stories. 3. Short stories. [1. Heroes—Fiction. 2. Cancer—Fiction. 3. Short stories.] I. Hale, Shannon, author. II. Condie, Allyson Braithwaite, author. III. Nielsen, Jennifer A., author. IV. Mull, Brandon, 1974– author. V. Diaz, Jonathan, editor, photographer.

PZ5.H757 2015

[Fic]—dc23   2015012627

Printed in China   05/2015
R. R. Donnelley, Shenzhen, China

10 9 8 7 6 5 4 3 2 1

❧

To Amelia Flamm

You changed my life completely.
May you continue to sing, design,
create, and inspire.

❧

Contents

INTRODUCTION

Thank you for your thoughtful purchase of this book. Because of you, we will be able to continue making dreams come true for beautiful kids facing the fight for their lives. You have given hope to a child who desperately needs it and for that I am truly thankful!

THE MISSION

The Anything Can Be project seeks to create lasting hope and raise awareness in the fight against pediatric cancer, one dream and one photograph at a time. I have been able to take the dreams of these cancer-fighting warriors and bring them to life through the power of photography. The photographs and the amazing stories that accompany them are meant to remind kids that they are full of power, strength, hope, and happiness.

To find out more about the Anything Can Be project, please visit our website at www.AnythingCanBeProject.com.

THE BEGINNING

In late 2013, I realized I was not satisfied with where my photography career was headed. I was proud of my work, but I also felt like it was missing certain meaning and purpose. I wanted to create art that meant something, that gave people a sense of hope and inspiration.

I have always been fascinated by the power and poignancy of a child's imagination. Children are not afraid to dream big; they believe anything is possible. They are innocent. With this innocence comes dreams and honest aspirations that, from the view of an outsider, might seem impossible. However, through the eyes of a child, such dreams are absolutely obtainable. I decided that I wanted to take this belief—this unadulterated hope in the future—and expand it through photography. I wanted to create art that could be used as a reminder to us all that dreaming big is good and that hope always exists.

Although all children's dreams are important, I wanted to focus my work on kids who could truly benefit from an image depicting their dreams coming true. With the uncertainty that cancer brings to a child's future, dreaming and holding on to hope becomes much more important. Dreams become more than just a passing goal; they become alternate worlds that can create an escape. Dreams become something to reach toward. Dreams create hope.

Children who fight cancer have become my ultimate inspiration—throughout this project, as well as in my life. Their cause has become mine, their hopes are now my hopes.

If you are interested in learning more about ways you and your family can be of service to children in need, please visit AnythingCanBeProject.com/serviceideas for links, information, and ideas.

THE BOOK

I wanted to create a book filled with powerful images of kids who are not only fighting cancer but also overcoming it through their dreams. I wanted a book that could serve as a way to inspire other kids fighting similar battles no matter where they live. Kids everywhere could open the book and find similar stories to their own.

But I wanted the book to be more than photographs. To that end, the Anything Can Be team assembled an unprecedented group of best-selling authors who have written wonderfully imaginative short stories as companion pieces to the artwork in the book. We are so honored and lucky to have these incredibly talented individuals writing stories for this book. Their contributions are priceless and make this book that much more unique and powerful as a tool for hope and awareness.

This book has been a labor of love for me, my team, and many others. I cannot think of a greater privilege than to be a part of this project and of the lives of these amazing kids. I hope that as you look through this book and read the stories, your imagination will take flight and you too will believe . . . *Anything Can Be.*

Jonathan Diaz
Creator and Photographer of Anything Can Be

LILLY

(Ewing's Sarcoma)

Meet Lilly! Lilly is the only known person to be born with Ewing's sarcoma and survive. She had a zero percent chance of surviving, yet she did. She is literally one of a kind. Nobody has ever done what she has done. She has had to fight tooth and nail for her life, and at three years old, she completely embodies what it means to defy the odds. She is an absolute miracle in every sense of the word. Her strength is matched only by her mother's. Lilly's story is as much about her as it is about her mother, who has stood by her and fought with her every step of the way.

Lilly is an example of never giving up hope, despite the odds. She is living proof of how powerful hope truly is and that anything is possible—anything can be.

LILLY, WARRIOR PRINCESS

Shannon Hale

LILLY WAS LOCKED UP IN A TOWER.

The first day wasn't so bad. She was too angry at herself for falling into her enemy's trap to notice the time.

The second day the anger still warmed her. The third day that heat began to trickle away. But the fight in her didn't.

She kicked the door again again again until sweat prickled her brow. She brushed her hand over her forehead and smooth scalp. The first thing her captors had done after shackling her in this room was shave off her hair. There were old stories, folktales of princesses locked in towers and their long hair granting them the power of escape.

It was utter nonsense, of course. As if her power was locked into her hair and could so easily be cut away. She laughed, alone there in the dark. Her power wasn't in her hair. It boiled in her blood, baked into her bones, strengthened with every breath.

Time and time again, the goblin army had tried to kill Princess Lilly until at last they realized the truth: she could not be killed. The best they could do was trap her, keep her locked up and helpless. But if she couldn't get out to help her people, then what was the use anyway?

She kicked the door again. It didn't even shake. She couldn't do this alone. She needed help. But how could anyone find her?

By the tenth day, a creepy crawling emptiness began to drip into her heart. She spent more and more time curled up on the floor, trying to sleep away the hopelessness. Her bones felt as cold as the stones.

On the eleventh night, she woke up with a start after a dream: she'd been old and wrinkled and still shackled in the same tower.

The world was as dark as mud. Like the dark, the hopelessness pressed in. She curled up tighter. How had she lost her will?

Lilly touched a stone. "Cursed. They cursed this place."

She'd read the stories. She knew what happened to princesses trapped in cursed towers. Eventually the hopelessness laid them down so low they slept forever, never waking again.

Her eyelids felt as heavy as the stones. She began again to dream. *Withered hands, brittle bones, her body just lying there like a fallen tree . . .*

"No!" she said, sitting upright. "I won't sleep!"

She cast her mind around for something powerful, some old magic she could cling to. Her mind and body were so weakened by the curse she could barely think. But a hum started on her lips. The song her mother used to sing to her when she was just a baby. A song sung every day until it had coated her bones and entwined with her muscles. A song so powerful only a mother could sing it.

Lilly hummed. She whispered. And soon she had the strength to sing.

As long as she sang, she was awake, the curse held at bay. So she sang for days. Her voice was hoarse. Her lips were dry. Still she sang. She just had to hang on until—

"Lilly!" a voice called from outside the tower walls.

"Yes! I'm here!" Lilly shouted back. "I'm in here!"

"Lilly! Hold on!"

The tower shook. Lilly fell, her knees bruising against the stones. The tower tipped. She covered her head with her hands. Everything crashed to the ground.

The wind was knocked out of her lungs. She coughed and gasped. Sunlight hit her like spears.

Strong hands lifted away the stones. And then they picked her up.

"Mother!"

Her mother carried her away from the tower. She sat in the grass and held her, rocked her, cried and kissed and even sang.

Lilly drank water from her mother's flask. She ate. And then she stood.

"You're exhausted," said her mother. "Rest first."

"No time," she said. "I can feel the ground shaking. The goblin hordes are on the move."

Her mother opened her mouth as if to protest, but shut it again and nodded. She, too, could feel the ground shake. She went to her horse—a tall, black stallion—and pulled items from the saddlebags.

"I've kept it ready," her mother said.

Lily's armor. She strapped on the well-worn leather jerkin, cap, and limb guards. They fit like a second skin, worn to a dark brown and smelling of sweet oil. She began to feel more herself.

The breastplate and helmet gleamed silver, like new money. Her mother helped attach the shoulder guards.

"I beat out the old dents," she said, "and shined it up a bit."

"Thanks," she said.

Her mother tied the breastplate in back and secured the helmet over her cap.

"I'll ride beside you," said her mother.

"I know you will." Lilly took her hand. "I'm not afraid."

"No, you're not," she agreed. "But *they* should be."

She looked around. Her mother had brought two horses, but neither of them was Arrow. The tower had stood on a hill high above the moors. The wind whipped from the east, tangy with marsh grass and a hint of brine.

"Arrow!" she shouted. "Arrow!"

"Lilly," her mother said, "didn't you know? Arrow was . . ." She couldn't seem able to say it. "We've looked everywhere, but when the enemy kidnapped you, they took Arrow, too—"

Still Lilly cried out, "Arrow!"

"I brought another horse for you," said her mother. "I know it's not the same, but—"

"She'll come," said Lilly. "I know she'll come."

The princess climbed atop a boulder, faced the wind, and shouted with all her might, "Arrow!"

A whinny. The clatter of hooves. A streak of white. Lilly hallooed with joy just as Arrow galloped by. Lilly leaped off the boulder, landing on Arrow's back. She threw her arms around the mare's neck, hugging her as they cantered together. When the horse slowed, Lilly slipped onto the ground, her arms still around the horse's neck.

"Good girl," she whispered into her mane. "Good, good girl. How did you ever get away from them, you clever pony?"

Arrow nickered and nuzzled Lilly's neck.

Lilly laughed. "That tickles!"

Arrow's nicker sounded almost like a laugh.

"We should go," said Lilly's mother. "The goblins . . ."

Arrow's nostrils flared as if she could smell the vile creatures on the wind. Arrow wore no saddle or bridle, but Lilly swung herself up onto her bare back, directing the horse with shifts in her seat, nudges of her knees and ankles.

They rode hard for hours. It had been days since Lilly slept. When she nodded off now, Arrow and the wind keeping her from falling.

At last they crested a hill and found the battle. Before the city walls stood her people, armed and fierce, fighting the goblin hordes. But for every one of her people there were five goblins, riding creatures with many limbs and yellow skin. They cackled and tossed smoke bombs and moved closer, ever closer, to the city.

"We're not too late," said her mother. "Thank the stars, we're not too late!"

Lilly pulled her sword from its scabbard. She raised it high, the sunlight flashing off its silver face. A hum almost too high to hear shot out from the blade. The battle paused. All eyes looked up.

"To me!" Lilly shouted, her voice echoing against the mountainside. "To your princess!"

There was a roar. Her people raised their spears and swords, clanged their shields, shouted her name. So loud was the clamor the very rocks in the mountain shook, the battlefield quaked.

The eyes of the enemy widened, large and white and, for the first time in many a year, showing real fear.

Princess Lilly charged.

SHANNON HALE

Shannon Hale is a *New York Times* best-selling author of fifteen children's and young adult novels, including the popular *Ever After High* trilogy and multiple award winners *The Goose Girl, Book of a Thousand Days,* and Newbery Honor recipient *Princess Academy.* She also penned three books for adults, beginning with *Austenland,* which is now a major motion picture starring Keri Russell. She cowrote the hit graphic novels *Rapunzel's Revenge* and *Calamity Jack* and illustrated chapter book *The Princess in Black* with husband Dean Hale. They live with their four small children near Salt Lake City, Utah.

http://www.squeetus.com

RAE

"Give yourself permission to dream." —Randy Pausch

KORBYN
(Acute Lymphoblastic Leukemia)

Meet Korbyn! Korbyn's dream is to be a firefighter because he wants to help people, just like so many have helped him. He has a kind and giving heart. For his photo shoot we were able to visit a local firehouse. Korbyn was able a take a ride in a big fire engine, practice his firefighting skills, and was made an honorary fireman. See more from Korbyn's photo shoot with the QR code!

A Fireman Always Helps

Tyler Whitesides

FIRE CHIEF KORBYN PULLED ON THE HORN, his bright red truck letting out a thundering peal as he came to a stop in the neighborhood. Pushing open the door, he swung down from the fire engine and approached a young boy standing on the sidewalk.

"You came!" cried the little boy. "Are you really here to help? I've got quite a problem."

"A fireman *always* helps," Korbyn said, adjusting his oversized helmet. His jacket hung loose around his small shoulders, dusted with a bit of soot from a previously extinguished fire. He glanced around the neighborhood, but there was no sign of smoke.

"What seems to be the problem?" Chief Korbyn asked.

The little boy on the sidewalk pointed toward a massive oak tree beside the house. "I was flying a kite," said the boy. "The wind changed directions and my kite flew straight into that tree and got stuck."

Chief Korbyn smiled. "Wait here," he told the boy. "I'll have your kite down in no time!"

Turning back to his bright red truck, Korbyn whistled sharply. Almost immediately, the black-spotted head of a large Dalmatian appeared through the truck's open window. The dog seemed to grin at Korbyn, his tongue dangling as he panted in the hot summer afternoon.

"Spotto," Korbyn said to his trusty dog. "We have a kite to save!"

Spotto, well practiced from their years together, knew exactly what to do. In a flash, the dog was sitting in the driver's seat, his paws expertly manipulating the controls to the telescoping tower ladder.

Korbyn sprang into position on the small bucket platform at the end of the ladder. Shouting commands to Spotto, Chief Korbyn carefully rose higher toward the great oak tree.

The bright green kite was almost camouflaged by the leaves of the tree, but Korbyn's sharp eyes noticed it immediately. The ladder came to a halt, and Korbyn reached out, easily plucking the stranded kite from its entanglement in the branches.

"That's it!" shouted the boy on the sidewalk. He clapped his hands in merriment as Korbyn carefully set the kite in the basket beside him.

"Happy to help!" Chief Korbyn shouted. But before he could tell Spotto to bring down the ladder, the boy on the sidewalk shouted again.

"While you're up there," he said, "if you don't mind . . . could you rescue my shoe?" The boy on the sidewalk stuck out his foot. Korbyn hadn't noticed before, but now he saw that the boy's left foot was covered only with a sock.

"How did your shoe get into this tree?" Korbyn asked, suddenly noticing the dangling shoelace among the branches.

"Before you got here," said the boy, "I thought I could knock down the kite. So I threw my shoe into the tree. But it got stuck."

Leaning as far as he could, Korbyn stretched out his fingers, grasped the tip of the shoelace, and gave it a tug. The shoe swung free, and Korbyn dropped it into the basket beside the green kite.

"I remember something else that got stuck up there," called the boy on the sidewalk. "Do you think you could rescue my cat?"

"How did your cat get up so high?" Korbyn asked. He'd rescued cats before, but not from such a height as this.

"You see," explained the boy on the sidewalk, "I threw my cat into the tree, trying to knock down my shoe."

Now that was an unusual use for a cat!

Korbyn turned his head, listening carefully beside the thick branches. All at once he heard it.

"Meow!"

"Come here, little kitty," Korbyn soothed, reaching into the branches until he felt the trembling furry pet. In no time, Korbyn was setting the orange cat safely into the basket next to the white shoe and the green kite.

No sooner had Korbyn set down the cat, then he heard an unexpected sound from the depths of the branches.

"Woof!"

His fireman helmet nearly toppled off as he leaned back in astonishment. "Is there a dog in this tree?" Korbyn shouted.

"Oh, yeah!" answered the boy on the sidewalk. "I threw the dog into the tree so it would knock down the cat!"

Korbyn shook his head in wonder, rising to his tiptoes and wrapping both arms around the shaggy brown dog. The animal was whimpering, terrified at such a height. Not Korbyn. He was used to being high in the sky on his fireman's ladder.

He scratched the shaggy dog behind the ears and placed it into the basket next to the orange cat, the white shoe, and the green kite.

The basket was filling up!

"You're doing great!" shouted the boy on the sidewalk. "I just remembered something else. Do you see my bike up there?"

Korbyn blinked his eyes in disbelief. Above his head, he saw the back wheel of the boy's bike spinning gently as a breeze passed through the leaves. Why was there a bike in the tree?

"Before you got here," said the boy on the sidewalk, "I was trying to knock down the dog, so I threw my bicycle into the tree." He shrugged helplessly. "And now it's stuck too!"

Chief Korbyn knew the bike was too high to reach from his current position. Whistling down, he shouted a few commands to Spotto. The loyal dog used his expert paws, maneuvering the telescoping ladder a little higher into the oak tree.

Korbyn had the bike. It was a shiny red one, and there was barely room in the basket next to the shaggy dog, the orange cat, the white shoe, and the green kite.

Chief Korbyn made it fit.

But the boy on the sidewalk wasn't finished. "Do you see my uncle up there?"

"Your *uncle*?" Korbyn shouted.

The boy below nodded. "I threw him up there to get my bike. But he must have gotten stuck."

"Yep," said a new voice from behind the leaves. "I'm stuck."

Korbyn parted the branches and saw a balding man propped sideways in the tree limbs. "I'm so glad you're here," the uncle said as Chief Korbyn helped him into the basket next to the shiny red bicycle, the shaggy dog, the orange cat, the white shoe, and the green kite.

The moment he saw that his uncle was rescued, the boy on the sidewalk shouted again. "Don't stop now! You're almost to the top! Tell me if you find the car up there!"

There was a car in this tree? "Unbelievable," Korbyn muttered.

"Don't act so surprised," said the uncle from the basket. "He only threw the car to try to knock me down."

Korbyn saw the automobile in the tree, but he couldn't reach it from where he was. A short whistle later, Spotto had once again maneuvered the ladder into the perfect place.

It was tricky to pull the car out of the branches, but Korbyn was an expert at such things. With just a few tugs, the vehicle came rolling down, balancing precariously on the edge of the basket next to the balding uncle, the shiny red bicycle, the shaggy dog, the orange cat, the white shoe, and the green kite.

Korbyn was exhausted, and he leaned down to see what the boy on the sidewalk might say next.

"You're really good, Mr. Fire Chief!" he said from below. "There's only one more thing stuck up there."

"What is it?" Korbyn asked.

"It's just an elephant."

"Just an elephant?" Korbyn shouted. In all his years at the fire department, this was the strangest rescue mission he'd ever attempted. An elephant? In a tree?

"I threw the elephant to knock down the car," explained the boy on the sidewalk. As if that were logical!

Korbyn saw the gray elephant perched in the topmost branches of the giant oak tree. Spotto raised the ladder to its highest height, but it wasn't high enough.

Chief Korbyn would have to climb.

Stepping off the ladder, Korbyn's tough fireman boots gripped the branches as he climbed toward the stranded elephant. His task seemed impossible, but Korbyn was an expert rescuer.

Taking the elephant gently by the trunk, he coaxed the big animal down through the branches until it landed in the basket next to the balancing car, the balding uncle, the shiny red bicycle, the shaggy dog, the orange cat, the white shoe, and the green kite.

Korbyn paused in the treetop, sitting in the highest branches and wiping sweat from his forehead. What a day!

He was just about to climb onto the ladder when he saw something far off in the distance.

Smoke!

There was a fire in the hills at the edge of town! He never would have seen it if he hadn't climbed so high into the oak tree.

Whistling to Spotto, Chief Korbyn leaped onto the ladder, and the faithful Dalmatian lowered him to the ground. There wasn't time to empty the basket or talk to the boy on the sidewalk.

In seconds, Korbyn was driving down the street, his overloaded basket of passengers bumping along in the afternoon sun.

Spotto honked the horn as the red truck screeched to a halt at the edge of the fire. Korbyn leaped into action, grabbing the hose and spraying a powerful stream of water into the bright wildfire.

Nobody was better at putting out fires than Chief Korbyn. He raced back and forth, spraying the hot flames until almost all of the fire had dwindled down to wet ashes.

There were only a few flames left, but Korbyn knew he had to extinguish them all. As he ran toward the remaining fire, his water hose snagged on the edge of a sharp rock, ripping it open and spraying water in every direction except where Korbyn needed it!

There was no way to put out the fire now! He needed a new water hose, but the truck didn't have a spare. Korbyn rubbed his chin in thought.

He knew just what to do.

Chief Korbyn raced back to the fire truck, climbing into the overflowing basket at the end of the telescoping ladder. Pushing past the green kite, the white shoe, the orange cat, the shaggy dog, the shiny red bicycle, the balding uncle, and the balancing car, he jumped onto the elephant's back.

They leaped from the basket and, at Korbyn's command, the elephant slurped up all the spilled water with its trunk. Then the little fire chief urged the huge animal forward. They raced bravely toward the flames and Korbyn shouted, *"Now!"* With one mighty blast, the big elephant sprayed all the water from its trunk.

The fire went out.

Korbyn leaned down and patted the elephant on the head. As he turned back toward the fire truck, he saw the boy standing on a sidewalk across the street. He must have followed them to the scene of the fire.

"That was wonderful!" the boy exclaimed. "You rescued my kite from the tree, *and* you put out a fire! Thanks for helping!"

Korbyn jumped down from the elephant and tipped his helmet at the boy. "A fireman always helps."

"Then maybe you could help me with one more thing?" The boy on the sidewalk rocked back on his heels. "While you were out here fighting the fire," the boy said, "I was playing with a paper airplane, and it got stuck in that big oak tree at my house. Could you help me get it down?"

Korbyn took a deep breath and straightened his fireman helmet. He nodded. "A fireman *always* helps."

TYLER WHITESIDES

Tyler Whitesides has always loved to write stories. He graduated from Utah State University with a degree in music. In addition to writing and music, Tyler enjoys fly fishing in the mountains, cooking, and vacuuming. He lives with his wife in Northern Utah. Tyler is the author of the Janitors series.

http://www.tylerwhitesides.com

WILLIAM

"Fairy tales are more than true: not because they tell us that dragons exist, but because they tell us that dragons can be beaten." —Neil Gaiman

JACOB
(Neurofibromatosis Type 1)

MEET JACOB! I first met Jacob in California at the Children's Hospital of Los Angeles. Jacob's tumor is located on his optic nerve, so unfortunately they cannot operate on it for fear of blinding him. They are monitoring its progression, however.

When I met Jacob, I was immediately struck by how confident and outgoing he is. His dream to be a motocross racer seemed to be very attainable for him. Jacob has an unconquerable spirit, and I have no doubt he will accomplish great things. If fact, he already has. Use the QR code below to find out more!

A Good Day for Victory

Jennifer A. Nielsen

Jacob! Jacob!" What had been a steady chant grew to a roar when Jacob's bike rolled into Dodger Stadium.

Dodger Stadium had hosted Supercross races before, so Jacob wasn't surprised to find himself surrounded by fifty thousand screaming fans. He also expected the five hundred truckloads of dirt that built up the jumps that would send his bike thirty feet into the air. Jacob planned to stay attached to his bike for all of those jumps. *If* he was lucky.

But this year's race was different. It was Dodger Stadium's first ever Mega Supercross, with a final lap designed to challenge the best racers in the world.

Jacob barely dared to look up at the final track, so maybe it scared him, just a little. But it scared him in the best way possible. His heart pounded with every second he had to wait to begin.

Jacob revved the engine as he smiled at the crowds. This would be a tough race, no doubt, but he'd fought battles harder than this before, and won. Yeah, he knew how to win.

Twenty other racers were here today, but as Jacob looked around the stadium, the signs being held by the fans all had his face on them. Everyone knew his name. They had all come to see him ride.

Colored flames burst around the stadium, signaling the countdown for the race.

If it was possible, Jacob's heart beat even faster than before. This was the moment he had dreamed of for years. When he was younger, and things were at their hardest, Jacob used to close his eyes and think of the sharp smells of dirt and gasoline. The sound of the cheers and bike engines blurred together in his ears. And the rush of blood through his veins told him the countdown was on.

Three . . . two . . . one! Applause erupted as Jacob's bike raced forward. The track was always crowded at the beginning, and three bikes to his right crashed together in one spectacular mess. He glanced over his shoulder to make sure everyone was safe. Luckily, they were all moving, and one big guy in green even waved a hand to tell Jacob to keep going.

Jacob took the first curve easily. It was a tight turn, requiring him to pivot the bike hard, but not hard enough to crash. He was younger than most of the other competitors and in fifteenth place. That wasn't a problem, though.

Words ran through Jacob's mind of what his family would say to him right now. "Just keep going forward," they'd tell him. "No matter what, you keep going forward."

And he did. The track had plenty of tight turns and a few great jumps, but Jacob sailed right through his first lap. He was getting close to another rider when he hit his first big challenge—a jump that required a sharp turn of the bike immediately upon landing.

Jacob drew in a breath. The nearest bike slid into the jump, and its rider rolled over the top. Jacob swerved to avoid him and launched awkwardly over the jump. His bike came down heavy on the right side, and Jacob's whole body lurched forward. The crowd gasped, certain that Jacob was about to fall, but he planted a leg down on the dirt and let the bike rotate around him. As soon as he was steady, he flew back into the race.

Jacob could barely remember the first time he raced. He was seven or maybe eight years old, but he took to his bike like he was born with a helmet on, ready to go. To him, motocross was freedom. It was raw power and strength and energy. It was victory.

When his bike surged past a couple others on the straight track, Jacob caught his first glance of his hero, nicknamed Stormrider. He was one of the greatest moto-cross racers in the world! And if Jacob wanted to know what it'd be like to race with Stormrider, then he needed to push even harder! That would take more than just speed. It required an uncommon courage. If there was any word Jacob understood, it was *courage*. He knew it; he'd lived it.

With the roar of the crowd surrounding him, Jacob began swerving in and out of the other bikes. Tenth place. Eighth place. Seventh. Fifth.

The other bikes in the lead were crowded together. Sure enough, Stormrider's black-and-white jersey was clearly visible, but there were plenty more bikers Jacob had to pass if he was going to take the lead.

One of the racers was a mountain of a guy almost as big as his bike. He wore a yellow uniform with a drooling bulldog on it. Mud spat out from Bulldog's tires and went everywhere. No, not everywhere. Pretty much just all over Jacob. The biggest splat went straight into Jacob's face and tasted gross.

Lesson learned: Don't smile while racing through mud.

The next part of the track had three jumps in a row, each one a little higher than before. Jacob was lighter on his bike than Bulldog and planned to use the jumps to get ahead.

Bulldog was first off his jump, but Jacob arched his bike high enough to get at least five feet of air. He came down only inches behind Bulldog. When they ramped up for the second jump, Bulldog swerved in front of Jacob, so even though it was a much higher jump, Jacob still only had enough speed for ten feet of clearance, not much different than Bulldog. The third one was the tallest. A long ramp could send Jacob as high as thirty feet. If he made it, he would come out ahead of Bulldog—and within reach of Stormrider!

Jacob grinned (and got a little more mud in his mouth), then revved his speed. A thirty-foot jump. He'd done his share of tricks before, but this was the biggest.

Ahead of him, Stormrider made a clean landing—of course. Two other bikers landed well too. Then there was Bulldog.

Jacob pushed his bike forward. He was already going fast enough to make the jump, but it wasn't about that. This jump was about landing ahead of Bulldog. Their two bikes left the ramp at almost the very same second.

"Aren't you afraid?" Bulldog shouted across at Jacob.

Jacob's grin widened. "I don't waste my life with fears. I just find the next challenge to conquer!"

And conquer he would.

Bulldog flew off the ramp and landed hard. His bike sank beneath his weight—literally sank into the mud about five feet short of the track and about halfway up his tires. He was out of the race.

Jacob made a smooth landing and revved his bike again for the next lap and the one after that. After a while, he lost track of how many times he'd been around the track, but it didn't really matter because he was slowly getting ahead of the others.

Suddenly, he was coming up on the last lap before the megacross track. Only two riders would be able to take it. Stormrider would be the first. Jacob planned to be the second.

He was already racing fast—they all were. What Jacob needed now was some old-fashioned muscling his way forward. Only one biker was between him and Stormrider, a guy with blond dreadlocks under his helmet and a Giants logo on his uniform. Jacob shook his head, more determined than ever. No way was he going to let anyone wearing a Giants logo win in Dodger Stadium!

Jacob's front wheel was nearly even with the other racer's back wheel. He edged to the right, forcing the nearest competitor over. Then he edged even farther right.

"You're gonna run me off the track!" Dreadlocks cried.

Jacob's grin widened. "Not off the track. Just into the ditch!"

And with one more nudge sideways, Dreadlocks was out of the race.

Stormrider glanced back at Jacob, and their smiles matched. "I knew it'd be you and me for the final lap," he called. "Are you up for it?"

Jacob revved his engine. "Bring it on!"

The final lap would first take them up a steep ramp to the upper level where the cheap seats were. Then it became a high-speed track around the perimeter of the upper stadium seats. The track was at a slight angle, meaning they'd have to keep their bikes going as fast as possible so they didn't roll off. Fire flares would ignite every twenty feet they rode, and at the end, the winning racer would have to jump his bike off the track, through a flaming loop, and land back on the ground.

Land *safely* back on the ground, Jacob reminded himself. His parents really wanted him to remember that safely part.

Jacob took his bike up the ramp, right behind Stormrider's lead. It was just the two of them—no other bikers had earned the right for this track.

Stormrider led out at top speed, and Jacob had to rev his engine once again just to keep up with his friend. His bike tilted slightly as they started into the long circle around Dodger Stadium, but Jacob had rarely felt so free. If he could ride through the air (well, almost), then nothing was impossible.

Nothing was ever impossible. He believed that.

"What's the hardest thing you've ever done?" Stormrider called back to Jacob.

Jacob shrugged. He'd done plenty of hard things. And maybe they hadn't been fun, but they'd made him strong—stronger than most kids his age.

"Well, listen carefully," Stormrider said. "Whatever it was before, that's about to change. The hardest thing you're about to do is ride through that flaming loop and then land on your feet. Don't slow down, don't lose courage, and whatever else, do not crash."

Jacob nodded. It was good advice for racing. Good advice for life. "Who's going through first?"

"We're going together. Are you ready?"

"I was born ready!" Jacob called back.

The crowd was nearly silent as the two racers approached the end of the track. A slight lip at the end gave them a jump into the air, and Jacob could feel all fifty thousand people in the audience holding their breath at once.

His bike launched, traveling through air, toward the fire. Suddenly the flame was all around him. The heat from it grazed his cheeks, but only for a second before he was through the loop and headed back to the ground.

Stormrider was focused on his bike, and Jacob did the same. He only looked up for a small moment to see his whole family at the end of the track, waiting to greet him.

Jacob's landing wasn't perfect. In fact, he hit hard enough that he almost bounced right off his bike and onto the ground, but he kept his grip on his handles and, somehow, kept his place on the seat.

But it wasn't until Jacob slowed his bike to a stop that he realized how deafening the stadium's cheers had become. Even the best Dodger's game was never this loud. No Supercross race in history had ever recorded such a celebration.

Over the microphone, an announcer was calling out that a new world record had been broken. A double jump through a flaming hoop, by Stormrider, and by a new world-record holder, Jacob.

"Those cheers are for you, kid," Stormrider said, winking at Jacob.

Jacob gave his helmet to his dad, then walked out in front of the crowd. He stretched out his arms, palms up, and did a full turn to the entire stadium. And then he took his bows.

Not his first win ever, and not the last challenge he would ever battle. But a pretty good day for a victory nonetheless.

JENNIFER A. NIELSEN

New York Times best-selling author Jennifer A. Nielsen was born and raised in Northern Utah, where she still lives today with her husband, three children, and a dog that won't play fetch. She is the author of The Ascendance trilogy, beginning with *The False Prince*; the Mark of the Thief series; and *A Night Divided*. She loves chocolate, old books, and lazy days in the mountains.

http://www.jennielsen.com/

CAMI
(Acute Lymphoblastic Leukemia)

MEET CAMI! Cami has battled cancer twice. She is one of the strongest kids I know. On the day of her photo shoot, her family received the wonderful news that, after a year of treatment and a bone marrow transplant, Cami was finally cancer free. It was a very good day!

Cami's dream was to be a fairy, but I am pretty sure her real dream was to finally be done with cancer. Her images depicting her as a strong beautiful fairy are meant to convey her conviction to take control of her life and fight the horrible disease that has plagued her body for many years.

I hope that when she faces tough times, she will look at her images and remember how strong she is.

Fairy Magic

Sara B. Larson

I CLUTCHED FROGGY TO MY CHEST A LITTLE tighter and tried to pretend I was somewhere else. Somewhere without pain or medicine or tests or cancer. In a garden, maybe, with sunshine radiating down, a warm, glowing blanket, and flowers and butterflies surrounding me in a whirl of color, and hummingbirds flitting beside me. Birdsong filled the air instead of the soft hum of the IV pump beside my bed. I pretended I was a fairy, like the ones I'd set up the home for in our real garden in the summertime.

Whenever I dared bring up my wish with Mommy, she always told me the same thing, "Anything is possible, Cami," with a little smile that made me wonder if she really believed that or if she was just saying it to make me feel better. Mommy does everything she can to make me feel better, but as hard as she tries, it doesn't always work.

But that night, I felt a flutter in my tummy that worked its way up into my heart, a tickle of hope that made me think maybe she was right, even if she didn't realize it herself.

"Anything is possible," I whispered to myself, watching the moonlight dance through the white curtains on either side of my bed and spread across the ceiling above me. As I spoke the words, the flutter turned into a flurry, urging my heart to squeeze harder, *beat-beat-beating* against my lungs, pumping the blood being made by my new bone marrow through my body.

I repeated myself, but this time a bit louder. "Anything is possible."

A speck in the darkness sparkled briefly, just a pulse of light, before it winked out again, leaving me breathless and half sitting upright in my bed.

Sure now that *something* was happening, though I had no idea what, I said it one last time, "Anything is possible!"

The glittery light pulsed again, this time bright enough to make me blink and turn away. When I opened my eyes, my entire room was glowing, an incandescent purple sheen that turned the air to liquid light, swaying and dancing around me. When I looked more closely, I saw one spot that was brighter than the rest, a deep, vibrant purple that pulsed so brightly I had to squint to see it. And that's when I realized it was coming toward me.

And that it wasn't just a light—it was a person.

Well, *kind* of a person. It was a tiny, glowing person with wings and skin that sparkled even in the darkness of night.

"Cami," she said, her voice much bigger than her tiny body. She spoke loud enough for me to hear, but not loud enough to wake my parents next door. "Do you know why I am here?"

I shook my head mutely, my eyes wide with wonder. And then it hit me and I gasped. I knew what she was—*she was a fairy.*

"My wish."

Her kind smile made me feel warm inside, like I'd done something to make her happy. "Yes, Cami, that's right. I'm a fairy."

"You . . . you're real?"

She came closer with a tiny flutter of her beautiful, glowing wings. "As real as you are." She smiled again. "My name is Michaela."

Up close I could see that her lips were purple too. Not the purple that mine get when I'm too cold or when someone can't breathe, but a light, beautiful purple, like a lilac.

"Put out your hand."

I did as she asked, holding up my hand with my palm toward her, my fingers out straight. Hardly able to believe this was real, I watched as she carefully landed, her bare feet tickling against my skin. I barely felt her; she weighed little more than a flower petal.

"Do you know what Michaela means?" she asked me, and I shook my head. "It means 'gift from God,' and that's why I'm here. Because God wants to give you a very special gift. Do you still wish to become a fairy, Cami?"

I stared at her for a long moment, my mouth hanging open, and then I nodded. "Oh, yes! More than anything." My hand shook with excitement and nearly toppled the fairy over. "I'm so sorry!"

"No, no, it's fine. Happens all the time." She laughed, a tiny, tinkling sound, as she regained her balance. Then Michaela looked up at me, her violet-colored eyes turning serious as she propped one tiny fist beneath her jaw. "You're a very special girl, Cami. You've been through a lot in your life."

I nodded, trying to ignore the pain that pulsed through my body even now.

"I have the power to grant your wish. I can turn you into a fairy—but only for one night."

Happiness filled me so completely there was no room for words. I could only stare at her in mute amazement.

Michaela smiled back at me, and then, with one last tickle, she fluttered her wings and lifted off my hand, hovering in the air just above me. With a flourish, she pulled a tiny wand out from behind her and twirled it in the air, creating a shower of purple sparks.

Warmth cascaded over me, cocooning me.

"Just say the magic words one more time," she instructed.

At first I was confused, and then it dawned on me—why she was here, why any of this was happening.

"Anything is possible!" I laughed in delight.

There was a flash of brilliant violet . . . and I was transformed.

Gone were my bed and my sheets and my nightgown and my IV and even the lingering pain from my most recent treatments.

I was floating over a beautiful lake. No, not floating. *Flying.* I was flying! With an involuntary burst of laughter I flapped my wings—I had *wings*—and shot across the lake, my reflection glimmering below me on the water. My dress was a beautiful shade of dark pink, and my skin sparkled just like Michaela's. I lifted my hands out in front of me, marveling at the beautiful sheen of my skin. Then I swooped down closer to the dark water so I could see my face better. I had *hair.* Long and thick—a brilliant, fiery pink, visible even in the darkness of nighttime. I wasn't swollen, I wasn't hurting.

I wasn't sick.

A bird called from somewhere nearby and I careened to a stop, flapping my wings madly to stay in place, spinning to try to see the bird. The beautiful melody sounded just like my friend Millie, who could do birdcalls. And then I saw it—a shimmer of green and blue on my left. A hummingbird flew toward me, her wings moving so quickly they were nearly invisible. She came closer and closer until we were only a few feet apart. We were nearly the same size, and as the hummingbird came to a stop and looked right at me, I swear her eyes looked just like Millie's.

"Millie?" I asked.

The bird couldn't respond, of course, but she flew around me, making me spin in order to keep an eye on her, and then she darted off, pausing for a moment to make sure I was following. I hurried to flap my wings and chase her down.

We danced across the lake, weaving back and forth, flitting toward the shore, where thousands of wildflowers swayed in the moonlight. When we reached the flowers, I heard the birdsong again, a familiar, lilting whistle, and I understood. Millie knew I was here, and she wanted me to know she was here too, in this place without pain or sickness or IVs or radiation or scans or chemotherapy. Here, where the night air was warm and the scent of flowers made the breeze a perfume that I inhaled deeply.

The hummingbird dipped lower, closer to the field, so that I could reach out and let my fingers skim the silken petals of the flowers we flew past. Ahead of us a doe and her fawn drank from a brook. They lifted their heads at our approach but didn't flee as they would have had I been my normal size.

Happiness built up in my chest, growing and spreading until it burst out of me in an uncontainable giggle that echoed back to me. The unseen bird whistled again, a happy chirping song, as the hummingbird and I chased each other through the magical, moonlit fields. On and on we flew, over brooks and streams, around trees, and across fields of lavender and magenta and golden yellow.

And then, just as the sky began to brighten, hinting at the sunrise to come, I spotted a flash of purple and paused. Michaela slowly flew toward me, holding her wand.

"Is it time already?"

"I'm sorry, but, yes. It's time to return home." Michaela came closer, but I turned to look at the hummingbird one last time. She circled around me, and then dashed off into the light of dawn.

Michaela murmured something beside me, and when I blinked it was all gone. The lake, the fields of flowers, my hummingbird, and the familiar whistle. I was back in my bed, but it was no longer the middle of the night. Outside my window, the sun was beginning to rise.

On my dresser lay a beautiful, glittering wand—only this one was a vibrant, beautiful pink, the exact color my hair had been. And beside it was an exquisite porcelain figurine of a blue-and-green hummingbird, exactly like the one I had flown beside all night long.

The night I got to have my wish come true—the night I had become a fairy.

SARA B. LARSON

Sara B. Larson is the author of the acclaimed YA fantasy novel *Defy*, and its sequels, *Ignite* and *Endure*. She can't remember a time when she didn't write books—although she now uses a computer instead of a Little Mermaid notebook. Sara lives in Utah with her husband and their three children. She writes in brief snippets throughout the day (while mourning the loss of naptime) and the quiet hours when most people are sleeping. Her husband claims she should have a degree in the "art of multitasking." When she's not mothering or writing, you can often find her at the gym repenting of her sugar addiction.

www.SaraBLarson.com

ANNIKA

(Neuroblastoma Stage 4)

Meet Annika! At two years old, Annika is our youngest subject. We created an entire fashion studio for her to play in. She was shy at first, but once she warmed up, she had a great time playing with all of the fashion designer props we had for her. She especially loved all the shoes—go figure!

Annika is very particular about what she wears. Luckily we came prepared and had two outfits for her to choose from because one of the outfits was not to her liking. The outfit she is wearing in the image was her favorite.

A quick note on the hummingbirds in the image. Like Annika, Millie Flamm was a young girl battling cancer—and an amazing fashion designer. I wanted to pay tribute to the little girl who helped inspire this project. So Millie is depicted here as the hummingbirds helping Annika fulfill her dream, a dream that Millie shared in life. See if you can find the hummingbirds in many of the images.

Annika, Little Fashionista
Kristyn Crow

On a starry night in Salt Lake City, Annika was born.

Instead of crying, she put on her momma's beads, stuck a flower to her diaper, and cooed.

Annika's daddy paced back and forth. "I think our daughter may be a fashionista," he said.

"A *fashionista*?" gasped Annika's momma. "How do we raise one?"

As Annika grew, so did her sense of style. She didn't just walk; she sauntered. She didn't just smile; she struck a pose.

Annika loved trying out new hairstyles in the bathtub. Like the beehive. And the mohawk. And the ducktail.

She used her building blocks to make a runway.

And she liked to wear long dresses with her toes covered up. "Look, I'm a mermaid," she'd say.

Every night at bedtime, Annika would bounce on her bed and declare, "Momma, Daddy, someday, I'm gonna be a *star* fashion designer."

"You're already a star to us," Daddy would say.

"But even little fashionistas have to brush their teeth and go to bed," Momma would add.

It wasn't long before Annika was designing clothes for her big sister, Lily, and all her friends.

"This dress has cap sleeves. And this one is appliqué," Annika said. "How do you like this lounge suit?"

"My little sister is the best fashion designer in the world!" said Lily. She and her friends loved wearing Annika's amazing designs. They would show up in their ordinary clothes and go home dressed like movie stars. Their parents were always very surprised.

Being a fashionista wasn't easy. Annika had to be very careful with her scissors and sewing needles. Sometimes hummingbirds would fly into her window and help her stitch and sew, just to make sure she was safe. They knew Annika was no ordinary little girl.

Every day when Annika woke from her nap, she would say, "Someday I'm gonna be a *star* fashion designer!"

"You're already a star to us," said Momma.

"But even little fashionistas have to pick up their toys," said Daddy.

One afternoon, a limousine pulled up to Annika's house. A movie actress, Sadie Simone, came to the door with all her bodyguards. "I need a fabulous dress to wear to the Oscars," she said. "Annika, I saw a design you made for my second cousin's daughter's niece. Dahhhling, please come to my mansion in Hollywood and design a gown for me!"

"I'll have to bring my Momma and Daddy," said Annika.

"Fine, fine," said Sadie. "Make me a dress and you'll be famous! You'll do shows at Bryant Park! Lincoln Center! *Paris, France*!"

Annika's eyes grew very big. Oh, how she wanted to be a famous designer. But Daddy and Momma weren't so sure. "It can be a tough world, even for little fashionistas," they said.

Annika gave them her fiercest diva-tude. "This is my dream! I'm gonna be a *star* designer! NOTHING CAN STOP ME!"

Momma folded her arms. Sometimes little fashionistas just had to learn things for themselves. "Then we'd better pack our bags," said Momma.

After a plane ride to California, Annika and her parents arrived at Sadie Simone's Hollywood mansion. It was the most beautiful house Annika had ever seen. There were fountains and winding staircases.

"This is your big chance," said Sadie Simone, "to design me a dress that will make you famous!"

Annika sketched the fanciest dress she could imagine. Then she went shopping with Momma and Daddy for the sparkliest materials she could find. She took measurements of Sadie while the actress was posing for the paparazzi. Then Annika went to work. Hummingbirds flew in the windows to help her.

SNIP SNIP SNIP went her scissors.

POKE POKE POKE went her pins.

WHIRRRRRRR went her sewing machine.

SNIP, POKE, WHIRRRRRRRR. It took many hours.

"*Voila*!" said Annika. "Sadie, here is your fabulous gown for the Oscars!"

Sadie Simone wrinkled her nose. She walked around the dress. "No, no, no. That's not right for me," she said. "It's the wrong color. And . . . too sparkly! It just won't work!"

Annika's measuring tape tumbled to the ground.

"I'll have to try another designer," said Sadie. "Now, out you go. I guess not everybody can be a *star* fashion designer."

Annika flopped down on her sewing box and began to cry. "I ruined my big chance!"

Momma picked up Annika's measuring tape and wiped her tears. "Sorry, honey. Even little fashionistas have to deal with rude people."

"Come on," said Daddy. "Let's go home."

When Annika and her parents arrived back home, Annika dove onto her bed and sniffled. And for a long time she didn't dream up any new designs. Or use her sewing machine. Not once.

Days passed. Weeks. Then one evening when Daddy was watching television, the Oscar Awards ceremony was announced. Big celebrities were all arriving for the event. The ladies wore their loveliest gowns on the red carpet. A TV reporter was asking them, "Who is your designer?"

"Prada," said one.

"Valentino," said another.

And suddenly there was a gasp, and everyone on TV stopped talking. Sadie Simone had arrived. Daddy, Momma, and Annika stared at the screen. "Hey!" Annika said. "She's wearing the dress I designed!"

"What a stunning gown," the reporter said to Sadie. "Who is your designer?"

"Annika, little fashionista," Sadie said. "She made me this gorgeous dress, dahhhling. At first I didn't like it, but then some crazy hummingbirds flew around my head and chirped at me until I tried it on. It was *sensational*! Oh, the fit, the glam, the glitz! It's the perfect dress!"

Sadie turned slowly around in place, and the paparazzi took so many pictures of her the television screen went white.

The next morning, the phone started ringing at Annika's house. It rang and rang and would not stop. Daddy said, "Celebrities keep calling. Movie stars. Annika, everyone wants you to design their clothes for next year's Oscars!"

Annika smiled. She dusted off her sewing machine. "I'll think about it," she said. "But right now I have to greet my *real* fans."

Ding-dong. All of Lily's friends had shown up to Annika's house. "Annika! Annika!" they cried. "We love your designs!"

"My sister is the best designer in the world," said Lily.

"Please design me a new outfit," said one friend.

"Something *fierce*!" said another.

Annika nodded. Then, like a true fashionista, she started creating new designs. Lots of hummingbirds flew in the window to help her.

SNIP SNIP SNIP.

POKE POKE POKE.

WHIIIRRRRRRRRRR.

When it was finally bedtime, Annika bounced on her bed. "Am I a star fashion designer *now*?" she asked Momma and Daddy. She pulled her nightgown around her legs like a mermaid tail.

Daddy kissed Annika on the forehead. "You've always been a star to us."

"And to *me*," said Lily.

"But," said Momma, "even little fashionistas have to . . ."

"I know," said Annika, getting her toothbrush.

KRISTYN CROW

Kristyn Crow is the award-winning author of numerous books for children, including *Bedtime at the Swamp, Skeleton Cat,* and the Zombelina series. She is also the screenwriter for Clark Planetarium's newest space adventure movie for kids, *The Accidental Astronauts.* Kristyn lives in Layton, Utah, with her husband, Steven, and their seven creative and musical children. This project is dear to her heart.

http://kristyncrow.com/

CAMI

"And above all, watch with glittering eyes the whole world around you because the greatest secrets are always hidden in the most unlikely places. Those who don't believe in magic will never find it." —Roald Dahl

MARLEY
(Acute Lymphoblastic Leukemia)

Meet Marley! Marley is the oldest cancer survivor in this book. She was diagnosed when she was eleven years old, but even then she was already dreaming of playing soccer in college. Before her cancer diagnosis, Marley seemed well on her way to achieving her goal. After her battle with cancer, the lifesaving drugs had taken their toll on her body, making it that much more difficult to play soccer.

Recently, Marley's dream of playing soccer in college came to fruition when she was made a member of the Idaho State soccer team. Marley is an example of someone who not only defeated cancer but is now actually living her dream.

MARLEY'S SHOT
Stephen Reid Andrews

MARLEY DROVE DOWN THE FIELD, DRIBBLING the soccer ball to the outside and then past the center halfback. Laura and Julie, the two strikers, were fanned out on either side so Marley could pass the ball to the wing if needed, but only the center fullback was between Marley and the goalie.

I got this, thought Marley.

"Pass!" yelled Laura, closing in on the goal from her left-wing position.

Marley rolled her foot over the top of the ball to fake the pass to Laura but then abruptly tapped the ball to the other side. The fullback stuck out her foot, but it was too late. The ball had already passed, and, like a graceful dancer, Marley hopped over the fullback's leg.

She had a clear shot at the goal. She only needed to outsmart the goalie. Turning her head to the left, Marley looked off the goalie, who instinctively took a step to her right. Incorrectly anticipating the shot, the goalie had fallen for the fake as had been Marley's plan. Marley pushed her foot toward the ball, connecting dead center and propelling the ball from her foot like a shot from a cannon. Though it seemed like the ball was suspended in the air for minutes, it only took half a second for it to reach the goal.

Marley watched in total disbelief as the ball bounced off the crossbar, springing back at a forty-five degree angle with such force that it cleared the goalie's box on the rebound. Marley's plant foot had slightly slipped before the kick, causing the error.

Without trapping the ball, Laura swooped in from the side and, cocking her leg back, put her force behind a kick. The ball went off her foot perfectly. As straight as a laser, the ball bounced forward. The goalie had no chance to stop the shot, and the whistle blew as the ball came to a rest inside the net.

The Eagles had won the state championship.

Immediately, the entire team mobbed Laura, tackling her to the ground with excitement. Teammates on the sidelines rushed onto the field, and students from the stands followed as the celebration intensified.

Marley joined the celebration, happy for the win and happy for Laura, but devastated that her shot had not been true. She couldn't stop herself from thinking that all the congratulations being showered on Laura should have been hers. She never missed that shot—in a hundred tries she would never miss. The shot was as routine as brushing her teeth. She had been inches away from being the hero. It should have been her.

She looked to the stands where she knew the recruiter from Idaho State University had been sitting. The recruiter had come specifically to see if Marley was good enough for Idaho State's team. The recruiter was no longer in her seat, and she was not on the field. Marley's shoulders slouched in defeat, and she felt like crying, though not for the same reason that her teammates were crying. Since the first time she touched a soccer ball when she was a little girl, she had dreamed of playing for Idaho State, but that chance had slipped through her fingers—two inches too far to the right. Her dream had been crushed.

Amidst the congratulations, the splashing of Gatorade, and the celebration of her teammates, she looked around for the next best thing. The recruiter from the University of Western Colorado had also been at the game. Marley spotted the UWC recruiter stepping onto the field. The recruiter, a slender woman with dark hair, was looking Marley's way and smiling.

Marley began to regain enthusiasm. It wouldn't be like playing at Idaho State, but at least it would be playing somewhere.

The recruiter started to walk toward her. Marley smiled and prepared herself, attempting to hide her previous disappointment.

"That was some shot," said the recruiter.

"Tha—" Marley began to respond, but her words were cut off as the recruiter walked passed her.

With more disappointment, Marley turned to see that the recruiter was talking to Laura, who had been standing behind her, preparing to squeeze Marley in a congratulatory bear hug.

"We came to this game for other reasons, and I'm glad we did," the recruiter said to Laura. "We would have never seen your talent. You are just the young lady we would like to have with us at UWC."

Laura couldn't hide her excitement, and Marley had to swallow her disbelief. Before today, not a single recruiter had been interested in Laura. Marley's miss had put Laura at the top of the list. Only inches to the left, and Laura wouldn't be at the top of anyone's list.

"Really?" said Laura.

"Yes. What do you say? There are a few other girls I was supposed to evaluate, but if you give me a verbal commitment now, I don't see the need for anymore evaluations."

Laura jumped up and down, grabbing Marley in her excitement. "Yes! Yes! Yes!" yelled Laura. "Did you hear that, Marley? I'm going to play for UWC!"

Marley's heart sank. That should have been her offer. The verbal commitment should have been hers to give. Laura didn't deserve the offer—Marley did.

Marley faked a smile.

Though Marley tried to be happy for Laura and the rest of the team, the celebration in the locker room was emotionally painful. The other girls begged her to attend the team party at the Doubletree Hotel, but she knew she couldn't go. Watching

Laura get congratulated and watching her talk about how excited she was to play for UWC would be too much.

To avoid the situation, Marley acted like she would catch up with the girls but instead drove to a place where she knew she wouldn't be bothered by anyone—a small, neglected park behind her home. She would often sit on the lone bench in that park when she needed to think.

Marley sat on the bench and cried until it was dark, replaying the shot she had missed in her mind a hundred times. When she couldn't cry any longer, she looked despondently into the night sky.

Eventually, a beautifully clear shooting star streaked across the sky.

What if that star was a sign? she thought. Though it seemed ridiculous, she couldn't help the reflexive impulse to make a wish on the shooting star. "I wish," she said aloud, making a childish plea, "I wish with all my heart that I could replay the last ten seconds of the championship game."

A more inexperienced soccer player would have wished to have simply made the shot, but Marley knew if she had a chance to retake that shot there was no way she would miss. She wanted to feel the euphoria of the shot going in. She wanted to experience the exhilarating joy she had seen Laura experience.

She buried her head in her hands, wanting to cry again, but as she pressed her palms to her eyes, Marley's head began to spin. She closed her eyes tightly and shook her head like she was shaking off a blow to the head. When she opened her eyes, she couldn't believe where she was. She was back on the soccer field. She was in the game. Her wish had come true, and she had been given a second chance.

"Marley!" called Julie as the ball went sliding in front of her. Julie had given her a perfect cross, allowing her to beat the center halfback.

"Pass," called Laura from the other side.

Like before, all that was between Marley and the scholarship to Idaho State was the center fullback, and, also like before, she disposed of the center fullback quickly, tapping the ball to the outside and hopping over the player's leg. This was it. She would not miss again. She could feel the excitement building inside her as if she had already made the shot.

A split second before she took the shot, out of the corner of her eye, she saw Laura approaching the goalie's box. Within that moment, an image flashed in her mind. She envisioned Laura's perfect happiness and the smile that had stretched across Laura's face as the UWC recruiter had extended the offer. She saw Laura jumping up and down in her excitement. Laura wasn't good enough to walk on to a college program. If Laura didn't get her chance now, she would likely never play competitive soccer again. Could she take that away from Laura? Could she be the reason that Laura's dreams would remain unfulfilled?

Marley did the only thing her integrity would allow her to do. Cocking her foot back, she aimed for the post, kicking the ball so it purposefully bounced off the post and back to Laura. As before, Laura was in perfect position to volley.

To Marley's absolute relief, Laura's foot met the ball, and the ball shot into the net like it had before. The whistle blew, and the Eagles won the game a second time.

This time Marley celebrated with the other girls, enjoying the moment. Everything happened as it had before. Everyone mobbed Laura for being the hero, and Laura got the scholarship to UWC. The only difference was that this time Marley was genuinely happy for Laura and the team. The fact that she wasn't the hero didn't mean her life was over.

And instead of going to the park, Marley attended the team party at the hotel. She was glad she did. Enjoying her teammates for a final time before graduation and taking part in the celebration was something she couldn't believe she had wanted to miss before.

As she finished her glass of punch and put the cup on the buffet table, she couldn't help but smile. Things were going to be all right.

A hand on Marley's shoulder got her attention.

"Marley?" said Coach Taylor.

"What's going on, Coach?"

"There is someone in the lobby to see you." Coach Taylor was smiling.

"Who?"

"You'll have to go see."

Marley rolled her eyes. With the way Coach Taylor was looking at her, she figured it must be a boy from school.

Reluctantly, Marley walked from the banquet hall to the lobby, hoping that the boy was at least somewhat cute. Her jaw nearly dropped as she saw the recruiter from Idaho State instead.

"Marley," said the recruiter with reserved excitement. "Thank you for taking a minute from your celebration. That was quite a game."

Marley looked behind her, thinking there was no possible way this recruiter was speaking to her.

"Yeah," Marley stuttered.

"I'm Cheryl Silver, the athletic director for women's sports at—"

"Idaho State," Marley interjected.

"Yes. That's right. I'm sorry I didn't speak to you earlier, but Coach Kay wanted to be here with me."

"Coach Kay?" said Marley with disbelief.

From down the neighboring hall, a well-dressed woman appeared.

"Marley," said Ms. Silver, "this is Coach Kay Williams, head coach of the Idaho—"

"Idaho State women's soccer team," finished Marley with even more excitement. She had done her homework on Stanford and recognized Coach Kay immediately.

Coach Kay stretched out her hand, and Marley shook it.

"I wanted to be the one to invite you to Idaho State," said Coach Kay.

Attempting to hold in her excitement, Marley wanted to pinch herself to see if she was dreaming.

"That is," continued Coach Kay, "if you haven't already committed to another school. I noticed the UWC recruiter at your game. You haven't already committed to UWC, have you?"

"No," said Marley, gathering her thoughts.

"Well, then, what do you say?"

"But I missed the game-winning shot today," said Marley skeptically.

Coach Kay laughed. "We've been watching you all year, Marley. We're not concerned with the one shot that you missed. We're more interested in the dozens you've made. One single moment may define a game, but it doesn't define a soccer player. So, what do you say?"

"Yes!" Marley squealed, charging Coach Kay and Ms. Silver for a hug they should have been expecting.

STEPHEN REID ANDREWS

Stephen Reid Andrews is the author of several acclaimed works including The Visions of David Palmer series, *Remnant of the Beast,* and The Bamberg Trials series. Stephen resides in the shadows of the red hills of Southern Utah with his wife and four children. His youth and young adulthood were scattered with creative works that evidenced his tendency to dream and tell stories, but not until 2011 did he discover his talent for communicating those dreams and stories through writing. He has been writing professionally ever since and will continue until the dreams and stories stop coming.

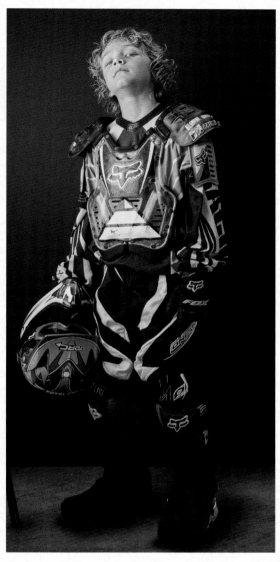

Jacob

"It's not the size of the dreamer; it's the size of
the dream." —Joshua Ryan Evans

Jordan

(Ewing's Sarcoma)

Meet Jordan! Three weeks after her father passed away, Jordan Kennedy was diagnosed with a very aggressive form of bone cancer. Jordan courageously fought with everything she had, but nine months after her diagnosis, Jordan found rest and peace.

This image was taken two weeks prior to her passing. She was in so much pain but wanted to make this image. Together she and I imagined a better place—a wonderland, where pain and hurt were not a worry, where she was perfect and healthy.

This is what we created together.

Jordan in Everywhere
Liesl Shurtliff

The day was warm and beautiful and perfectly boring until the fish walked by.

Jordan sat on a blanket by the lake, feeling quite pitiful.

"Jordan! Come play!" Her sister laughed and splashed in the water, but Jordan was too tired for laughing or splashing.

"Would you like to play a game, Jordan?" Her mother had a stack of board games and puzzles, but Jordan had grown tired of all of them.

"No, thank you," she said. "I think I'd just like to rest."

Truthfully, she wished she could play games with her father. He could make a wonder out of anything, even chores and schoolwork and eating vegetables. He could even make sad things turn inside out and become happy, but he was gone now. She missed him.

She wove a crown out of the clover near her blanket and placed it on the head of her Siamese cat, Bouncer. Bouncer pawed at the crown, then ate it.

"There's a saying about eating one's crown," Jordan said. "Or is it eating one's hat?" Jordan's father had always told her it was a good idea to use words and phrases in a sentence to see if they sounded correct. She tried it. "If a fish walks by, I'll eat my hat." It sounded correct, even though she knew it was a ridiculous sentence.

However, at that very moment, a fish did indeed walk by. He was a rather large fish, nearly as big as Bouncer, and he walked on the tips of his tail fins. In his left fin he carried a cane while his right fin was occupied with a monocle. Jordan squeezed her eyes shut and opened them. The fish was still walking.

The fish was walking toward the lake. Of course. Fish lived in lakes and ponds and rivers. That much made sense. Bouncer crouched low as the fish walked right by them, and then he pounced and gave chase. The fish adjusted his monocle and glanced back. When he saw Bouncer, he let out a sort of shrill gurgle and broke into a run. The fish was quite fast for a fish out of water, though Jordan had no reference for how fast a fish *should* be out of water.

In no time at all, he had reached the edge of the pond, and Jordan could not run fast enough to catch up, so she called to him in the off chance that a fish with a cane and a monocle might understand English.

"Oh, Mr. Fish!" she cried.

The fish did not respond. He tapped the water with his cane. The water began to swirl. The fish dove into the funnel and was sucked down.

"Wait!" said Jordan, but it was too late. The fish was gone, and now she would never know where he was going. Except Bouncer was not ready to give up. As soon as the fish had jumped into the water, Bouncer pounced after him.

"Bouncer, no!" Jordan cried. She snatched Bouncer just in time, pulling him to safety, but in the process she lost her balance and tumbled headfirst into the water. She made a small splash and was sucked down, swirling faster and faster in the vortex.

Bouncer meowed pitifully down at her.

"Don't worry, Bouncer! I'll be right back!"

It got very dark and then very bright, and she felt she was going up rather than down, though that couldn't be right. That would defy the laws of gravity, and she knew very well that when something was dropped it would go down, not up. And yet she felt as though she were going up. She supposed facts and feelings were altogether different things, but the fact of the matter was she could see a bird swimming in the pond.

"I didn't think birds could swim," she said to herself, "except penguins, of course, but they don't swim in ponds, nor do they live anywhere near here. They live in Antarctica. Or is it the North Pole? No, I'm certain it's Antarctica." But she wasn't certain at all. She had learned a great many facts in school, but sometimes they got jumbled, so it was difficult to be certain of anything.

The bird soared through the water, beating its wings. It joined with a whole flock of birds and they flew in a flying J, which Jordan thought quite a nice change from a V.

Jordan continued to fall, or rise, whatever the case was. She saw a great many curious things in the water, including a bouncy ball, and tap shoes that tapped. She even saw a plate of chocolate chip cookies and was tempted to try one, except she didn't think they would taste very good, being in a lake. The last thing she saw was a Chihuahua driving a small car. The dog honked the horn as though he wanted Jordan to get out of the way, but where could she go? She was still going down—or up—and the car was going mighty fast, right toward her.

Jordan reached her arm through the spinning water and—

Shleeooooop!

She was sucked out of the water and tumbled onto dry ground. The car came too. It burst from the lake and landed right beside her.

"Oi!" barked the Chihuahua. "You need to watch where you're going! You can't just swim in the middle of a road, you know."

"But I didn't see a road," said Jordan. "It's a lake. There aren't any roads in lakes. Besides, cars don't drive in lakes, only boats do."

"Boat?" said the Chihuahua. "Boats are for flying."

"Then what are airplanes for?" asked Jordan.

"Swimming," he said. "Everyone knows that. Now get out of my way. You're in the middle of an intersection."

Jordan looked around. She saw no intersection, just grass and trees and rough walking paths.

"I don't see how this can be an intersection."

"Well, you'd better open your eyes," said the Chihuahua. "If you don't pay attention you could go in quite the wrong direction, or worse, you'll remain in the same place and never go anywhere."

"Where is there to go?" Jordan asked.

"Everywhere." The little dog honked his horn and sped off through the trees.

"Well," said Jordan, "you don't see that every day. But I suppose he's right. I can't just sit here forever. I need to find Bouncer, and I had better move before I'm run over by a turtle on a motorcycle." She was laughing at her silly imagination when something burst through the lake and sped by her with a roar. Jordan was splattered with a fair amount of mud, but she could see well enough to make out a motorcycle and the distinct outline of a turtle shell on the back of the bike. Its head was pulled down into its shell.

"I don't think that's at all a safe way to drive," said Jordan.

She started walking back toward the house, but when she got to the place where the house was supposed to be, it was not there. Instead she found the fish, the turtle, and the Chihuahua gathered around a table with a large cake in the middle. Jordan's stomach grumbled to remind her how hungry she was.

"Hello," she said. "Might I join you?"

"That depends," said the turtle. "Do you wish to shrink or grow?"

"Grow, I think," said Jordan.

"Then you may not," said the Chihuahua. "This is a shrinking party only. We're all shrinking ourselves."

"Why would you want to shrink?" asked Jordan. "Being small is such a hardship."

"Not necessarily," said the fish, who put his monocle up to his eye to observe Jordan. "If you grow, you might become bigger, but then everything around you becomes smaller. However, if you shrink, then everything else becomes bigger, so really, the more you shrink the more everything else grows, and that's the greater feat."

"I suppose you're right," said Jordan, though she wasn't sure at all. All she knew was that she was hungry, so she sat at the table and cut herself a slice of cake. She took a bite. It was delicious. Chocolate. She took another bite, and this time it tasted of strawberry. The next bite tasted of roast beef and carrots, which might not sound quite right for a flavor of cake, but it tasted perfect.

She felt a curious tingling sensation in her fingers. A buzzing started in her ears. The fork in her hand was getting bigger. It was as big as her arm, then as big as her leg. It kept getting bigger until she could no longer hold it. The table was getting bigger too, and her chair, the turtle, fish, and Chihuahua, until she realized that nothing was getting bigger. She was getting smaller.

She got smaller and smaller until she was surely no bigger than a mouse. Everything around her had become so large that she could see things she hadn't noticed before, like all the little ridges in the grass, and the web of roots in the ground, and the man walking in the distance who looked incredibly like her father.

"Dad!" she called, but he did not hear her. Of course not. She was too small, but she couldn't let him get away. She had to go after him. She walked to the edge of the chair. It was too high to jump, and the legs of the chair were rather straight and smooth, so there was no possibility of climbing. Besides, even if she could get down, there was no way she would be able to catch up with her father. Not at this size.

"I think I'd rather be a bit larger than this," said Jordan. "How do I grow larger?"

"Eat less cake," said the turtle. "You just ate too much. If you eat less, then you'll grow, because less is more and more is less."

"I'm not certain that makes sense at all," said Jordan, but she found a crumb of cake on her jeans and ate it anyway. This time the buzzing in her ears came first, and then the tingling. She grew up and up, past the table, past the fish, turtle, and Chihuahua. She grew above the trees. The lake was nothing more than a pond, and the party below her looked like a set of toys.

She searched for her father. She thought for certain being as big as she was she would be able to see him quite clearly, but that was not the case. Everything was so small she couldn't tell what was what.

"Come now!" said the fish. "There's no need for such gluttony. You ate far too little!"

"When I eat too much I shrink, and when I eat too little I grow into a giant. When I'm small I see too much. When I'm big I can't see enough."

"That just goes to show that bigger is not always better and more is sometimes less," said the fish.

"How can I make myself a normal size again?"

"You must take neither too little nor too much," said the turtle, "but just the right amount."

"And how am I to know if I am taking just the right amount?"

"You can't know, silly creature," said the Chihuahua. "You're supposed to have somebody else serve you. For example, I gave a slice of cake to the fish, and he gave a slice to the turtle, and the turtle gave a slice to me, and now we all have the right amount."

"Well, then, would you be so kind as to serve *me* the right amount?"

"You're so very large, I do believe you'll have to eat the rest of the cake to shrink down to proper size." The fish reached out a fin and pushed the cake toward her. Jordan reached down and took the cake between her fingers. It was more the size of a small cookie. She ate it and tingled and buzzed and shrunk back down to her proper size.

"And now we're out of cake," said the turtle.

"I'm very sorry," said Jordan. "Shall I make you some more? I'm actually quite good at making cake."

"Goodness, do you want us all to disappear? You can't make us *more,* only *less.*"

"Of course," said Jordan. "I will make you less, but I'm afraid I must go now. Good-bye! Thank you!" Jordan left the inside-out, upside-down cake party and ran in the direction of her father. She found a lovely little path going through the trees and thought for certain it must be the path her father was on.

"Dad!" Jordan called. She saw him just as he turned around a corner of the path.

"Dad! Wait for me!" She ran along the path, but when she turned the corner, her father was nowhere in sight.

She was determined that she would find him. It seemed impossible that he should be here, and yet it had to be him.

"Everything has been impossible here," said Jordan, "from the walking fish to the driving Chihuahua to the shrinking and growing. So why would I not see my father, too? It's the least strange of all of them." But the faster she went and the more she looked for him, the farther and farther away he seemed to become and the fewer and fewer glimpses she saw of him, until Jordan was ready to give up entirely.

Jordan sighed. "Everything is upside down and backward here. Perhaps if I try to get lost, I'll find a way home."

Jordan stepped off the path. She wound around the trees and hopped over logs and stones until she came to a meadow. It was full of dancing dandelions. The wind rushed, and the dandelion fluff rose and danced in the air. Her father once told her that each dandelion fluff was a wish. Jordan closed her eyes.

"I wish . . ." She made one wish a thousand times, but she didn't say it out loud. It was too deep and close to her heart, so Jordan lay down in the grass and closed her eyes. She let the dandelions and wishes wash over her.

"Jordan," said a voice. It was very familiar, the voice of laughter and joy. It was the sound of comfort and home.

"Dad?" said Jordan. She opened her eyes. She sat up, and there was her father. He looked just as she remembered except the sun surrounded him in such a way that made him all the more real and alive.

He held out his hand to her. "Will you come with me?" he asked.

"Where are we going?"

"Everywhere," he said.

"Is it very far?"

"It's so close, most people miss it."

"I've missed you," said Jordan.

"I am quite easily missed," he said with a smile. "But now I am here and so are you, so we should not waste our time missing anything when we can discover everything." He tipped his head up toward the sky. Jordan took her father's hand and they went Everywhere together.

LIESL SHURTLIFF

Liesl grew up in Salt Lake City, Utah, the fifth of eight children. She loved dancing, singing, playing the piano, and reading books. Today she lives with her husband and three children in Chicago, which is a wonderful city except that it is decidedly flat and very cold in the winter. When she writes, she often wanders back to her childhood and gathers the magic that still remains. She hopes to share that magic with children everywhere.

http://lieslshurtliff.com/

Sarah

(Acute Myeloid Leukemia)

Meet Sarah! Sarah dreams of becoming an astronaut and space explorer. She is also one of the most outgoing and sassiest cancer fighters I have ever met. She has dealt with countless difficulties, including staying in the hospital for more than three hundred days. Sarah is also the recipient of a lifesaving bone marrow transplant. It is amazing to me that some of us carry lifesaving cures to cancer. So cool!

Sarah is from Montana but travels to Salt Lake City for treatments and doctor appointments. In November 2014, she was in Utah for a couple of days so we took a day for her photo shoot. You can see some behind-the-scenes images from her shoot by using the QR code below.

67

Swimming in the Stars
Ilima Todd

22:04 31.7.2917 Cryo Tank #36: Initializing Cognizant Restoration

My eyes open, but it's still dark. I cannot see.

I am blind.

I blink and blink and blink. Nothing but blackness. My eyelids struggle to lift and close. Something heavier than air presses down on them. I panic when I realize water engulfs my eyes, my face, my body.

I am drowning.

My mouth opens, but my scream remains caught in my throat; my lungs are engulfed by this water as well.

That's when I feel the cold. Raw. Biting. It's an impossible cold. I shouldn't be alive or aware feeling this kind of cold. I finally remember, as though the cold has slowed the flow of my thoughts. I'm not blind, and I'm not drowning.

I am swimming in the stars.

An image of my mother appears. A memory.

She stands on the shore of a lake with a towel in her hands. "Come back," she calls to me. "Sarah, it's too cold. It's time to come in."

"Just one more minute," I say, arching my back and extending my arms and legs as I float on the still lake. It's dark out, and the stars reflect on the quiet water, making me

feel as though I'm floating among the constellations. I tilt my head back and close my eyes, silently wishing I really was up there in space, weightless, drifting in the emptiness without this planet holding me down.

A roaring sound jolts me from my calm, and my feet drift down to settle in the muddy foundation of the lake. I look across the water to the launching station, to the slender form of the spacecraft, the fiery jets propelling it into the air. I watch until it breaks through the atmosphere and casts a blazing streak through the dark night, like a shooting star. I make a wish that I'll be chosen soon. That I'll finally get my chance to launch into space like others before me.

When I finally step out of the water, Mom wraps me in the towel.

"Did you see the spacecraft?" I ask, my teeth chattering. "That's the sixth one today. They're leaving more often now." Dozens of people are aboard each one, settling into their cryo tanks for the hundred-year journey.

"Yes," Mom says. "I saw it." Rubbing her hands up and down my arms to warm me, she adds, "Don't worry. We're not meant to stay here. We never were. This planet can't keep its fingers wrapped around us forever. It'll be our turn soon, Sarah."

I follow her gaze to the bits of dust and debris left in the spacecraft's wake, multiplied in the reflection of the lake. They fall to the surface, left behind like the rest of us. I hope my mother is right. I hope I won't have to wait much longer to really swim in the stars.

The memory slips away, along with the water that surrounds me, draining to leave me shivering in the dark of my cryo tank. I still can't see, but I turn to my side anyway, coughing up the remaining liquid oxygen inside me. When I inhale this time, it's air that enters my chest, and it burns. Collapsing onto my back, I bring a hand to my chest and will my lungs to move under my direction—breathe in, breathe out. After a few minutes, my lungs remember what they're meant for, and the burning isn't as severe. But I continue to shiver in the frigid cold.

I hear a whisper, as though someone has let out a small sigh, and a thin stretch of light surrounds me as the roof of my cryo tank lifts open, breaking away from its seal.

Warmth floods me immediately, making me shiver again, but this time with relief. I sit up, my muscles protesting every movement, while my eyes strain to adjust to the light of the room. It's as though every part of me has forgotten its intended function and needs a minute to remember.

When I can finally focus, I see the familiar interior of a spacecraft. It is compact and utilitarian, meant for a singular purpose: a one-way trip to a faraway planet. I slip out of my cryo tank, sparing a moment to steady my feet. Identical tanks line up alongside mine, but none of the others have opened yet. I run my finger along a metal label on the lower half of my tank: *Sarah Magera*. Liquid drips from my bodysuit to the floor, but I'm too excited to care that I'm making a mess. If I'm awake, then that means . . .

I hurry to the port side and walk to the front of the ship, looking for a viewing window to see outside. But the walls are covered with metal and wire or glowing buttons. One button catches my eye: ARTIFICIAL GRAVITY. The side of my mouth rises, and I only hesitate a moment before I press the button.

Everything begins to rattle, like a space giant has tapped the side of our ship to see if anyone's inside. My entire body vibrates, and it reminds me of another memory from home.

"It's starting," I say, pulling on Mom's arm. "We're going to miss it."

She smiles and drops the shirt she's been folding, following me out the front door. We get on our hands and knees and crawl into the cardboard box I've fashioned into a space-craft, modeled after the one about to take off across the lake.

"Hurry." I roll onto my back and make room for her. "We have to finish our launch prep." I pretend to strap myself into my imaginary seat.

"Ten," Mom says. "Nine . . . eight."

I press the make-believe buttons in front of us. "Fuel—check. Oxygen—check."

"Seven." Mom pulls her hands down the sides of her face as though securing a helmet to her shoulders. "Six . . . five."

I do the same and then reach for her hand to squeeze it. "This is what we've trained for," I whisper. "We're ready."

Mom squeezes back. "Four . . . three . . . two."

I hear the roaring of the real spacecraft in the distance and imagine the sweet anticipation of those on board. I try to mimic it—beads of sweat form along my forehead, and my heart races in my chest.

"One."

I press my body into the ground to imitate the g-forces at work. The ground vibrates in reaction to the real launch. And when it finally stills, I close my eyes and envision the black of space surrounding me.

Home is swept away from my mind like a handful of dust. Except my planet isn't home, is it? Not anymore.

The rattling stops. Slowly my arms feel lighter and hover beside me, and when I press off the floor, I drift into the air, floating in the cramped quarters of the ship. My yellow hair sticks out all over the place without gravity telling it what to do, and when I touch the fabric of my suit, water droplets scatter away in all directions, swimming with me among these stars.

I stretch out my arms and legs, arch my back, and close my eyes, basking in weightlessness. No anchor. No ground to hold me back, no water to keep me afloat. This is the opposite of drowning. It is drifting in particles of light and space. It is life.

I tilt my head back and open my eyes, half expecting to see a spacecraft shooting into the atmosphere, but then I remember I'm on that craft now. I've already shot into the sky. I've already broken through the atmosphere and stretched across the black night. I am the star some other girl has wished upon.

I kick myself toward the port front and extend my arms to stop myself near the gravity button. I press it again, and slowly my body lowers to the floor of the ship. I run my fingertips along the rest of the buttons and pause at another one: OBSERVATION WINDOW. I press it, and the entire roof of the ship begins to retract. Thick glass separates me from the universe. When the retraction stops, so does my heart. Because there, filling the entire window, is the most beautiful planet I've ever seen.

I studied photographs of this as a child.

I endured endless lessons about it in school.

Rumors have been passed down through generations.

But none of it does the planet justice. I am swimming among the stars, but for the first time in my life, I want to be anchored. I want to be on that ground more than anything.

"How long will it take?" I ask, tugging on the collar of my bodysuit.

Mom smiles, brushing a strand of hair out of my face. "You know it's a hundred years, Sarah. You've always known that."

"No," I say. "I mean . . . how long will it feel like?"

She glances around the interior of the spacecraft that will be our home for the next century. "It will feel like you've woken from a long nap. And the life you've lived before will be a fleeting dream compared to what awaits us, to what will be within your grasp when you wake."

I lie back and settle in place inside my cryo tank. "I wish we could spend a little while in space," I say. "While we're awake, I mean. I wish we could live among the stars instead."

"No, Sarah. When you see our new home, you'll want to be there as soon as you can." Mom leans over and kisses my forehead. "It's where we came from. Where we belong. Where we're meant to be."

"I love you, Mom."

She pats my cheek and steps back from my cocoon. "Love you, Sarah."

The cryo lid moves into place, and everything goes dark.

I can already feel it, the pull this planet has over me. It mocks the confines of this ship, knows it owns me before we've even met. I reach an arm upward, wanting to shake its hand. I long to know what it feels like to walk along the green grass. To run my hands through the blue water. Feel the wind that commands the wispy white clouds through the sky.

I don't know how long I stand there yearning for something so close yet still out of reach. Until . . .

"You're awake."

I drop my arm and turn to the familiar voice. "Mom?" My own voice shakes, and I wipe the tears that trickle down my face.

"Oh, sweetheart." She steps toward me in her damp bodysuit and buries me in her embrace. "Welcome home, Sarah." She glances at the window roof and smiles. "Welcome to Earth."

ILIMA TODD

Ilima Todd was born and raised on the north shore of Oahu and dives for octopus with her dad every time she visits—otherwise she's diving into books in the Rocky Mountains where she lives with her husband and four children. She graduated from Brigham Young University with a degree in physics and eats copious amounts of raw fish and avocados without regret. But mostly she loves being a wife and mama and wouldn't trade that job for anything in the world.

http://ilimatodd.com/

CARSON

(Acute Lymphoblastic Leukemia)

Meet Carson! In May 2012, Carson was diagnosed with acute lymphoblastic leukemia (ALL), but his dream is to be a bull rider and a cowboy. During our photo shoot, Carson rode a horse for the first time. It was a special moment and something he will never forget.

Carson's nickname is "Tuff Boy," and it definitely fits. One of the things I admire is the unconquerable spirit these kids have as they face the fight for their lives.

To see some behind-the-scenes images as well as get a glimpse into how I made this image, use the QR code below.

Cowboy Carson

Jess Smart Smiley

It used to be such a lovely place.

People would travel long distances to vacation here . . . but not anymore. The town that used to be paradise no longer existed.

There were no rainbows of colorful flowers left to sniff. No gushing cascades of water spilling over rocks and bubbling until they stretched out and flowed into perfect rivers and streams. No more hills covered in soft green grasses to catch you when you fell and to whisper in your ear as you gradually fell asleep. There were no more birds to fill the air with melodic thrums and trills, whistles and warbles. Even the wind seemed to have gone.

It used to be such a lovely place.

What used to be a bright and hopeful city, filled with people and a beautiful, sprawling landscape, had become a desert. People no longer bothered to say the name of the town out loud, because it wasn't worth saying. It wasn't worth thinking about. Everything in the town was dirt and dust and sand and grit. Everything looked the same, smelled the same, and felt the same, because it was the same.

One dry and dusty day (which was every day), a bicycle wheeled into town. The tires screeched to a stop, and a pair of cowboy boots hit the ground.

"Oops," the boy said to himself, looking at the dusty dirt that seemed to be endless.

Carson was lost.

He made a face and turned around, trying to remember how he'd ended up in this nameless desert.

Carson scratched an itch on his leg through his blue jeans and removed his large, ten-gallon hat, waving it in front of his face. The sun suddenly seemed much hotter and drier than ever. Carson struggled to swallow, feeling a pinch in the back of his throat. (Cowboy clothes were fun to dress in, but they could be hot!)

After adjusting his giant silver belt buckle, Carson straddled his "horse" (which is what he called his bicycle) and started pedaling.

It was no use—he was lost. Trapped in an endless desert. He had no way of knowing which way was home or even how far away home was.

Carson thought of his family and wondered if he'd ever see them again. He tried not to cry, but the tears came too quickly.

Suddenly—a sound.

"Mom?" Carson wiped away his tears and blinked, but he saw no one.

"Mom, I'm over here!" He jumped and waved his arms. Carson turned in a circle, but his mother was nowhere to be found.

Again, he heard the sound.

Carson squinted, put on his hat, and then squinted again.

Far, far away, in the dusty distance, Carson thought he saw something. He leaped to his metal steed and pedaled as hard and as fast as he could.

He was getting closer. Closer.

Carson couldn't quite tell what had made the sound, but it was the only thing that wasn't dust for miles around. He was getting closer.

The something seemed to be moving.

"Mom! I'm coming!"

Carson was filled with a burst of hope as he sped across the dry ground. The something was coming into view.

"Mom?"

Closer.

"I'm right here!"

Closer.

Then, all around him, an explosion boomed and knocked Carson to the ground. He blinked hard and shook his head, propping himself up by his arms.

He glanced to his side to see that the explosion had come from his bicycle tire, which had blown apart. The pieces rested next to a hard, ancient cactus.

Carson frowned.

As he looked around, he noticed something strange.

Carson blinked, then leaned in, wiping at the dust with his hands.

It was a patch of grass.

It was covered in dirt, but it was grass just the same. He pushed more dirt away to find that the grass beneath it rolled down into a luscious hill with a house at the bottom. Carson couldn't believe his eyes! He ran back up the hill and confirmed that everything else was still covered in dirt.

"There must be a whole town under here!"

Carson thought of all the houses and hills that were sure to be covered in dust, and he felt dizzy, wondering at how such a thing could have happened.

He sat down next to his bicycle and noticed something else on the ground. There were footprints—*giant* footprints—all over the desert floor. Carson squinted as he realized they were not human footprints, but—

A flash of hot air blasted the back of his neck, and Carson wheeled around to find himself face-to-face with an enormous bull!

The blast blew his favorite ten-gallon hat right off his head, but Carson couldn't grab it. He was stunned. He was paralyzed with fear. The bull was terrifying. This must have been what he'd seen in the distance, what had made those strange noises.

Carson had seen dozens of bulls before, but this was by far the biggest.

Towering over him like an angry black fist, the muscular bull seemed to boil inside its skin, glaring at Carson with all the rage of a thousand thunderstorms.

Carson looked at his bicycle, wondering if he could ride away fast enough, but he noticed a torn piece of tire next to him. Without his tire, he was stuck.

As if reading his mind, the bull raised its gigantic left leg and threw down its hoof, crushing Carson's bike.

Carson whimpered. He was stuck in an endless desert, cornered by the largest bull in the world, without a single person to save him.

He thought of his family and prayed they would be all right.

The bull kicked up a cloud of dust, and the ten-gallon hat caught Carson's eye. As the dust circled up and around the furious bull, Carson felt a bolt of strength surge through him.

He grabbed his hat and stood up, adjusting his belt buckle and tightening his hand-carved wooden bolo tie. Carson shouted into the tumbling cloud of dust, "I ain't goin' down without a fight!"

Pulling the hat over his head, Carson leaped into the whirlwind, disappearing in the swirling dust.

All around them the desert was dry, dull, and unremarkable. The desert went on for miles and miles, all of it nothing but flat, dusty earth. Except for Carson and the bull.

An enormous cloud of dirt spun around the two as Carson grabbed on to the bull's back and pulled himself higher onto the bull's neck. The bull fumed, snorting and grunting, spinning and spinning around, kicking up even more dust.

As the bull stomped, the dry ground beneath it broke open, revealing small patches of lush, green grass.

The bull's eyes glowed with red madness until Carson thought the beast might burst with fury. Instead, the bull continued bucking and kicking, knocking the dust from the earth, and building what became a violent, swirling tornado of dust around him. Carson clutched the bull's neck with one hand and held his hat in place with the other. The bull bucked wilder and wilder, but Carson held on, and, suddenly, the bull slowed down.

While the dust continued to circle and settle around the two, the bull lowered its head in submission. Carson had tamed the gigantic beast.

"Yeeeeeee-haw!" Carson shouted, waving his hat.

As the bull drew in large, slow breaths, Carson looked around and was amazed to find that the bull had kicked so hard that it had lifted the dust from the area. What used to be dry, flat ground was now an entire town, complete with rolling hills and beautiful homes—all without their former dusty disguises.

With the dust lifted, Carson was able to identify a few buildings in the distance that were near his home.

"Hi-yah!" he shouted, nudging the bull forward with his boots. The bull snorted and charged forward, the giant dust cloud still circling around them. "This way!" Carson pulled the bull sharply to the right, and they tromped down a familiar road. "Almost there." Carson laughed, his eyes filled with delight.

"Stop!" Carson shouted, and the bull screeched to a halt. "See that?" He pointed to an empty lot near his home. "That's where I'm gonna make my rodeo stadium. When I'm bigger." The lot was covered in rocks and mud. Seeing the ground now somehow made Carson sad, but the bull snorted an enormous snort, which blew the dust cloud right into the yard, covering the giant stones and muddy pools.

As the dust settled, Carson realized that the land was now the perfect place for a rodeo stadium, and he began to laugh.

"Carson?" He looked down to see his family looking up at him, worried. "You're okay!"

"Of *course* I'm okay," Carson said. "I'm a cowboy!"

With all of the dust now gone, people quickly moved back into the town. Children played in the streams and rolled down the hills. The town was even more beautiful and green than it had been before. But still, the town had no name.

As the mayor watched Carson and his bull race their friends on their bicycles, a thought came to him.

The next day, he gathered all the townspeople in the square and in a loud voice declared, "I hereby name this town—Carson City!"

Carson beamed, his family cheered, and even the bull gave a snort—that sounded a little like a laugh.

JESS SMART SMILEY

Jess Smart Smiley is a writer, illustrator, and graphic designer living in Utah. His publications include *Upside Down: A Vampire Tale* (Top Shelf Productions, 2012), *Rumpus on the Run: A Monster Look-n-Find Book* (Mascot Books, 2013), and *10 Little Monsters Visit Oregon* (Familius, 2014).

http://jess-smiley.com

CAIMBRE

(Neuroblastoma)

Meet Caimbre! When a tumor was found in her abdomen, Cambria was diagnosed with neuroblastoma. Her dream of becoming a mermaid is fitting since she lives in California. Her photo session was so much fun to shoot, and she had no problem getting into character. She was such a professional it was like she had been posing for years.

The hardest part of her photo shoot was finding the right background for some of her pictures. Shooting in California, we thought that would be easy. But we didn't have a lot of time to find the right location, so we started visiting California beaches to find the right combination of rocks, waves, and light.

Our last beach was Laguna Beach, and it happened to be the perfect location for the photo on page 95. Caimbre's beautiful expression, full of hope and life, perfectly embodies what this project is about.

THE MERMAID'S TALE

Lehua Parker

W E'RE DOOMED," RORY THE CABIN BOY MUTTERED, clinging like a barnacle to the ship and searching the sea below. Rogue waves crashed against the hull of the *Winter Nomad,* stinging his eyes and burning the back of his throat. "Two lanterns on the bowsprit, and I can't see a thing. This fog is thicker than oatmeal and twice as sticky."

"Boy!" roared Master Azi from the helm. "Are the western shoals afore ye?"

"I don't think so, Master! I can't see the harbor buoy nor hear its bell." Rory flinched as a fresh wave drenched him

"Keep your eyes peeled, Rory. We've got to be close," Captain Northwind said. "Can you see lights on shore?"

"No, sir. But I'll keep looking."

"It's no use, Cap'n," Master Azi said. "I daren't bring the *Winter Nomad* closer to shore. We've no choice but to head out to sea until the fog lifts. The Seawitch has beaten us."

Along the mizzenmast a seagull skipped a jig.

"Azi, we aren't giving up," Captain Northwind said, snapping his spyglass closed. "We've battled ogres and pirates, crossed the Forbidden Sea, and journeyed to Chasm's Portal and back. It's not yet midnight. This war isn't over."

Back on the bow, the smell of iced lemonade and sunshine cut through the brine to tickle Rory's nose. "Achoo!" He sneezed. "Caimbre?"

"There are easier ways to take a bath than hanging from a figurehead," she teased.

Rory squinted and waved a hand in front of his face, chasing the fog away. At the edge of the lanterns' light he spotted her long blonde hair and the wake of her mermaid's tail. "Caimbre, this is not a joke. We're in trouble. The Haven Port lighthouse is dark, and we can't find the passage through the reef."

"Humans worry too much. The fogbank isn't big. Hold your course steady and you'll be clear in two shakes of a tuna's tail."

"No, Caimbre, we won't. This fog never thins. It's surrounded us since sundown. The closer we get to Haven Port, the thicker it gets. It's not natural."

Caimbre tossed her hair and narrowed her eyes. "You think it's the Seawitch. But why would she bother?"

"We found it, Caimbre."

"The antidote?"

Rory grinned. "It's in the captain's quarters. Seen it with me own eyes."

"You did it! Princess Leona and her kingdom are saved!" Caimbre clapped her hands and dolphin-danced on her tail.

"But only if we get the antidote to the castle before midnight. If we fail—"

"Then Princess Leona sleeps for a thousand years and the Seawitch rules instead." Caimbre groaned, sinking in the water to her chin. "You're right. You're doomed. This fog is part of the Seawitch's plot."

"You could help us," Rory said.

"Me? I'm nobody."

"You're exactly the hero we need. Can you climb to the top of the lighthouse and light the signal fire?"

"Climb?" She squeaked. "I've never even walked!"

"But you can, right? I mean, if you have to."

Caimbre fingered her starfish necklace as she bobbed in the water. *It hurts,* she thought. *Mother warned me that making legs burns like the fire of a thousand eel teeth in your tail.*

"Yes, in an emergency I can walk," she said. "But you don't need me. Keeper Merriweather lights the signal fire."

Rory pulled his chin to his chest and ducked as another wave washed over him. "But tonight he hasn't. Something happened to him; I'm certain of it. Otherwise he'd never leave a ship alone at sea in the dark."

"The Seawitch again." Caimbre slapped the water with her tail.

"Rory!" Captain Northwind shouted. "Report!"

Rory opened his mouth and swallowed a gallon of seawater. "Please, Caimbre," he sputtered. "Master Azi sent me to watch for the channel in the reef, but the fog is too dense. If the lighthouse isn't lit soon—"

"The Seawitch wins."

"And she'll sink the *Winter Nomad.* We'll be scuttled on the bottom of the harbor."

"The Seawitch would sink her?"

"To get the antidote she would. And she'd lock us in chains and put us to work in the salt mines."

"The salt mines!" Caimbre shot to the tip of her tail and whispered in his ear. "You should flee, Rory! Turn and sail as far and as fast as the wind will take you. Don't let her trap you like a crab in a net."

Rory shook his head. "We won't abandon our princess or her kingdom. Our entire journey has been a quest to save us all."

"But if you fail—"

"We fail or succeed together, Caimbre. Otherwise what was the point?"

Caimbre sank down into the water. Lying on her back, she looked up at Rory clinging to the figurehead and shivering. Her hair spread like a sea fan as she slowly beat her tail to keep pace with the ship.

Rory wants me to walk on land to save his ship and the kingdom. If Mother's right, each footstep burns like jellyfish blisters. The weight of climbing stairs will make the pain worse, but how much? Worse than stingray spines through a fin? Fire coral under scales? Whatever it is, it's going to be bad.

But how much pain will everyone suffer if the Seawitch rules? asked a new tiny voice inside. *You have to help!*

Caimbre nodded to herself. It was time to pick a side. She took a deep breath.

"The Seawitch can't win," she said. "Not when you've come so far."

"There's still time for us to get to the castle by midnight if you light the signal fire."

Caimbre flipped to her side. "I'll do it, Rory, for you and the *Winter Nomad*." With a swish of her tail, she turned from the ship and disappeared in the fog.

"Thank you!" called Rory.

Don't thank me yet, Caimbre thought, heading toward the lighthouse.

A few more flicks of her tail fin and the mist thinned to reveal the lighthouse breaching like a whale against the cold night sky. From the shadows of the dock, Caimbre craned her neck all the way to the arched windows at the top. *It's so far.* She shivered.

A seagull landed next to a mooring post, flapping his wings with a squawk.

"Easy for you to say," Caimbre sniffed, pulling herself out of the water to sit on the dock's edge next to him. Leaving her tailfin fluttering in the surging tide, she reached up and twisted the water out of her hair. She paused, her hand resting on the starfish pendant around her neck.

This is ridiculous. I can't remove my necklace and grow legs. Princesses and sleeping curses. Ships and magical fogbanks. Human problems belong to humans.

But the Seawitch isn't human, said the little voice inside. *And Rory asked you for help.*

It's too much. He doesn't know what he's asking, she argued.

But we have to do hard things, Caimbre. We have to think of others. That's what separates us from creatures like the Seawitch.

It will hurt.

But only for a moment. You have to try.

I'm afraid.

It's okay to be afraid, said the voice. *Heroes never think they're brave.*

Before she could stop herself, Caimbre swung her starfish necklace up and over her head.

"Eeerok!" screamed the seagull.

Lightning tingled along the tip of her tail and then shot like a bullet to her belly. Wisps of steam glowed as her green scales shimmered and popped. Toes bubbled out from her tail fin as it split into ankles, knees, and thighs. Holding her starfish necklace in a white-knuckled grip, Caimbre bit her lip and tasted blood.

I can do this, she thought. *But what if I can't?* She bit harder and held on. *The time for choosing is over. Enduring is all that's left.*

When the rending ended and the world stood still, she emptied her lungs in a rush and wiped the tears out of her eyes.

A thousand eel teeth, Mother? That was more like a million fishhooks!

The seagull grunted and cocked his head.

"What are you looking at?" Caimbre snapped. "Never seen a mermaid grow legs before? This is nothing. Stick around. For my next trick, I'll waltz with a penguin. Get ready to applaud."

The seagull rolled his beady eyes and sighed.

Looking down at her hips and thighs, Caimbre gasped. She wore a gossamer skirt with funny bulges along the sides. Rummaging in the pockets, she pulled out two stubby flippers. "Shoes? Mother, you amaze me. Your enchantment thought of everything." She turned the flippers over and peeked inside the openings, eyeing the space against the size of her new feet. "At least I hope these are shoes."

Running a hand along her calf, she shuddered at the dry, dull texture of her new skin, so different from its normal iridescent sheen.

Hair? Ugh! It's not enough that I've lost my beautiful scales, now I'm fuzzy, too? She shook her head. *Stop it. Pay attention to what matters. Rory and the others are counting on you.* Tucking her feet into her shoes and her starfish necklace into a pocket, she concentrated on slowing the hammering of her heart.

Across the harbor, the Haven Port bell tolled the hour. Caimbre held her breath and counted. Eleven bells! It was almost midnight.

I have to hurry. She looked at her lap. *But how do you move a leg?*

Seawater swirled around her feet and rose in a swell to kiss her knees. *Knees! That's it! Human babies crawl. I just have to get to my knees!*

Rolling sideways to her stomach and scooting like a seal, Caimbre dragged her legs onto the dock. *I've traded being sleek like a dolphin for being clumsy like a walrus. A fat, landlocked walrus.* She surveyed the distance to the lighthouse door and gritted her teeth. *Don't think, just move. One hand, one knee, just like a turtle.*

The dock rasped sharkskin-rough against her skin, but she persevered and soon came to the path that led to the lighthouse door. Caimbre paused, then gingerly pressed her hand against the gravel, testing it. Sharper than a bed of crushed beach glass, it bit into the flesh of her palms with the eagerness of a rabid barracuda. She scrunched up her nose. Crawling wasn't going work anymore.

I have to stand and walk or my skin will shred like seaweed in a storm.

The seagull waddled alongside her, yawning while she fought to pull herself upright against the mailbox.

"So, I'm boring you, Mr. Seagull?" she gasped, finding her balance on two feet. "Don't worry. This next part is better."

Six tottering steps brought her to the lighthouse door. Caimbre frowned. She had never opened a door before. She pushed. Nothing, not even a creak. Near the door's edge was a shiny metal knob that looked important. She poked it with a finger. When it didn't bite, she wrapped her hands around it, pushing and pulling with all her might. The door jiggled a little but held firm. Defeated, she leaned her forehead against it.

There must be an opening spell, she thought, *something that keeps evil out.* "Please, door, let me come in!" she whispered. "I promise I only want to help!"

The seagull landed on the open windowsill and chuckled.

"I don't see what's funny about this," Caimbre said.

An offshore breeze billowed the curtains like sails, startling the seagull. "Rooc!" he squawked and threw his wings wide.

"That's it! You're a genius, Mr. Seagull. I'll climb through the window!"

"Errk," mumbled the seagull as he hopped past the curtains and into the room.

The bushes around the lighthouse looked like lace but cut like coral as she hoisted herself through the window. "Ooofff!" she grunted, falling to the floor. She ignored her scratches and bruises. "Keeper Merriweather?" she whispered.

The hearth fire was only coals, but there was enough light to see Keeper Merriweather seated at his kitchen table, his nose smashed flat in a plate of potatoes and gravy. "Keeper Merriweather!" Caimbre shouted, scrambling like a crab to his side.

"Snnnnuugghle-blaaaht," he snored.

"Keeper Merriweather?"

"Shhhhuggngle-whannnnat."

Caimbre lifted his face out of the gravy and laid his head gently on the tabletop.

"Mushumummble," he said, but didn't open his eyes.

"He's out cold," Caimbre said to the seagull. "It's an enchanted sleep."

The seagull shrugged and nibbled on the loaf of bread.

"I'll have to light the signal fire myself." She spotted the pile of torches. "That must be how Merriweather does it—he lights a torch and carries it up the stairs." She plunged the tip of the longest torch into the coals and watched it flame like dragon's breath. "I can do this." She stumbled to the stairs. "I think."

Gripping the torch in one hand and the railing in the other, Caimbre raised her foot to the first stair. Pain shot from her heel to her heart, skewering her like a marlin's spike. "Oh!" She wavered, counting her heartbeats until the pain eased.

This would be so much easier if I could swim. A flick of my tail and I'd shoot through this tower faster than a shark in a feeding frenzy. She studied the turns in the stairway as it wound its way to the top. *It's like the spirals of a seashell. I'll pretend I'm a hermit crab making my way one twist at a time.*

At the forty-second stair, the world went blurry and the air turned thick. Caimbre started to panic. *What if I can't do this? It hurts too much. I should stop this madness and go back to the ocean where I belong. I could be home safe in my grotto with my tailfin on ice and a lovely mug of hot squid ink in my hands. No one would know I quit. Rory would think I tried but that the Seawitch beat me.*

Caimbre hesitated, her hand lingering over her starfish necklace.

No, she thought. *I would know the truth. All of this pain and hardship is only for a moment.* She patted her starfish necklace through the pocket. "Don't worry," she said. "I'll be wearing you soon."

Onward she climbed, each stair piercing deep as an sea urchin's spine into the sole of her foot.

Conquering the final stair, she didn't stop to cheer but shakily moved past the landing. The fresh breeze ruffled her dry hair, and she gulped the air greedily into her lungs. High in the top of the lighthouse and far above any remnants of fog, the night was clear. Starshine and moonlight streamed through the windows to reflect off the big mirror next to an unlit pile of wood.

"Carah!" the seagull said, swooping through an open window to land next to the wood.

"Show-off," Caimbre said. "Did you get enough bread, you greedy thief? That was Merriweather's supper you ate." She wobbled to a window. "Oh!" she breathed.

To the south of the lighthouse all of Haven Port and the harbor spread like seafoam rising to meet the castle on Nob Hill where Princess Leona slept. Turning north toward the open sea, Caimbre spotted a black cloud riding low over the water. "Pearly shells!" she spat. "The *Winter Nomad* is headed straight for the western shoals!" Quickly, she thrust her torch into the heart of the woodpile.

The seagull blew it out.

"What? That's impossible!"

The seagull twitched and shook like a bowl of sea cucumbers, wobbling and bobbling until he exploded in a whirlpool of feathers.

"Aha!" cackled the Seawitch as tendrils of smoke curled around her bulbous figure. She raised a tentacle and tapped Caimbre's nose. "Silly mermaid, did you think you could defeat me?"

"Seawitch!" Caimbre sputtered. "I should've known. Real seagulls have better manners."

"Oh, my," the Seawitch chortled. "If you could've seen yourself." She batted her eyelashes and pursed her lips. "Oh, I don't know, Rory," she simpered, "I *think* I can!"

"You, you—"

"Witch?" she cackled. "You should call me queen. There's no way the princess will get the antidote now." She grabbed Caimbre's arm. "Come. I'll show you how it ends. If you behave, I'll be kind and put you to work next to Rory in the salt mines."

"No!" Caimbre wrenched away and swung her leg in a roundhouse kick to the Seawitch's head.

It passed right through.

"Ooof!" Caimbre fell, the wind knocked out of her as she landed in a twisted heap next to a bucket.

"How deliciously delightful!" the Seawitch cooed. "The entire fate of the kingdom rests on a useless mermaid in a lighthouse tower." She flicked a feather off her dress and onto the signal pile. "Let's go. I don't want to miss the look on Captain Northwind's face when his ship crashes into the rocks. I'm done playing games with you."

Caimbre reached into her pocket. "It was never a game, Seawitch," she said. "But you're still going to lose." Tossing her starfish necklace onto the wood and looking to the night sky, she opened her mouth and sang.

A siren's song of a sea star called to a sky star, and a spark leaped down from the heavens, igniting the wood with a whoosh. The flames licked hungrily as the signal fire blazed with the light of a thousand suns. The mirror focused the light into a beam that raced through the darkness, scattering the fogbank and revealing the *Winter Nomad*.

"That's not fair!" the Seawitch said as the smell of burning feathers filled the lighthouse. "Mermaids can't call fire!"

Caimbre smiled. *But I did. Though I didn't know I could until I tried.* Bracing herself against the wooden bucket, Caimbre stood and peered out a window.

Captain Northwind wasted no time. The white sails unfurled, and the *Winter Nomad* raced away from the reef, sweeping past the entry buoy into the harbor. Even before the ship's lines were secured, people began scrambling down rope ladders to waiting horses and coaches.

Caimbre clapped and bounced with glee. "They're going to make it!" she said.

The Seawitch shrieked as she roiled and gurgled back to her seagull self. Giving herself a quick shake, she leaned forward to fly.

"Not so fast!" Caimbre reached down and tipped the wooden bucket completely over the seagull.

"SQUORK!" The bucket rattled and hopped as smoke steamed from underneath.

Caimbre sat on it. The bucket continued to shake and rock, but Caimbre just laughed. There was no way the Seawitch could escape.

Hours later when the horizon was shell-pink in the sky, the Harbor Port bell rang in jubilee, startling Keeper Merriweather awake. He thundered up the lighthouse stairs smearing gravy and mashed potatoes all along the walls. "Miss?" he asked when he reached the top.

"Oh, it's nice to meet you, Keeper Merriweather. I'm Caimbre, a mermaid."

"But you have legs."

"Temporarily. Oh, and I've also got the Seawitch trapped under this bucket."

Keeper Merriweather rubbed his eyes. "This feels," he said, "like the start of a very interesting day."

Turning to the signal fire, Caimbre crooked her finger, and as cool as its ocean home, the starfish necklace jumped out of the flames and onto her palm. "Let's go," she said, slipping her necklace back into her pocket. "With Keeper Merriweather here, going down the stairs will certainly be easier than coming up!"

LEHUA PARKER

Lehua is the award-winning author of the Niuhi Shark Saga trilogy for middle-grade and young adult readers and writes Lauele Town Stories and other works for adults. Originally from Hawaii and a graduate of The Kamehameha Schools, after a lifetime of travel and adventurous careers, she is currently an author, editor, public speaker, soccer mom, and project manager—not necessarily in that order.

Trained in literary criticism and an advocate of indigenous cultural narratives and diversity in literature, Lehua is a frequent speaker at conferences and symposiums. She lives with her husband and children in the high desert mountains of Utah.

http://www.lehuaparker.com/

CAIMBRE

"Dreams save us. Dreams lift us up and transform us." —Superman

SOPHIA
(Acute Lymphoblastic Leukemia)

Meet Sophia! The thing I love most about Sophia is how happy she makes everyone around her feel. You can't help but feel good when she sends one of her infectious smiles your way. But Sophia is so much more than her personality. It only takes a second in her presence to realize that Sophia has a majestic soul meant for greatness. Her struggles are beyond comprehension for most. Not only does she have cancer, but she also suffers from a serious heart condition as well as Down syndrome. Nothing seems to deter Sophia, though, as she lives each day to the fullest.

When her mother said that Sophia's dream was to read a lot, I was a bit perplexed as to how I should create her image. A picture of someone just reading a book wasn't as magical as I wanted it to be. But if we could get into her head to see what her imagination was doing—that would be cool!

This image is the result of a ton of trial and error before I got something I was truly happy with. I felt Sophia deserved an image worthy of her beauty and strength!

97

Sophia's Wings

Sharlee Glenn

IN A LAND FAR OFF AND LONG AGO, THERE WAS A kingdom inhabited only by birds—large birds, small birds, garden birds, water birds, songbirds, nesting birds, perching birds, wading birds. There were kiskadees, falcons, flamingos, and meadowlarks. Bluebirds, blackbirds, chickadees, and ravens. Swallows, starlings, swans, and yellowthroats. It was a peaceful kingdom ruled by a king and a queen—nightingales, both—who were much loved for their goodness and the sweetness of their songs.

The kingdom was called Volaria, and it was a happy place. All day long the trilling and chirping of songbirds could be heard. Snow geese and swans glided on the still waters of the land's many lakes. Eagles and falcons stretched their wings against the blueness of the sky as they soared, twisted, glided, and dove through the air.

The king and queen lived in a palace high above the valley floor. They were very happy, almost perfectly so, but they lacked one thing—a child. As the years passed, their longing for a child grew and grew. There was a doctor in court—an old raven named Dr. Ebon—who had lived in the palace since before the king was born and had served the king's father.

Dr. Ebon tried every method known to bird to help the king and queen, but to no avail. Then one bright spring morning, quite unexpectedly, the queen laid a single egg—smooth, glossy, and the palest pink. The king and queen were overjoyed. The king hovered as the queen tenderly cared for the egg and kept it warm. Dr. Ebon attended as the egg hatched and a beautiful baby nightingale was born—a girl. They named her Sophia.

To the adoring mother and father, baby Sophia was perfect in every way. But Dr. Ebon pushed them aside and swooped in to examine the baby.

"Something is not right," he said. "Do you see how the left wing is withered? She will never fly. We must bind the wing tightly to her body to protect it and to protect her."

The king and queen were alarmed by the urgency in the doctor's voice, and they allowed him to bind the wing.

"It is for the best," said the old doctor as he gathered his things and left.

But the tight binding pained the little bird. The queen could not bear to hear her cries, so she unwrapped the wing, covered it with kisses, and gently massaged it.

Little Sophia cooed and smiled up at her parents.

As Princess Sophia grew, the goodness of her heart became apparent. Though bound to the earth and unable to use her fragile left wing, she never complained— unless her parents taped the wing to her side, which they never did unless Dr. Ebon was around, and even then she merely let out the tiniest of sad chirps. Otherwise her disposition was as sunny as the brightest of summer days, and her kindness as constant as the stars in the heavens. Everyone in the palace loved her. And, oh, her song! It was as sweet and pure as golden honey.

The princess seemed content for the most part. Still, it stabbed her parents' hearts to see her watch longingly as the other birds flitted about and flew. She especially yearned to see the marvels that lay beyond the palace walls. The other birds would tell wondrous tales of their adventures and the vistas they witnessed as they flew about: great, crashing waterfalls, snowcapped mountains that sparkled in the morning light, valleys as green as emeralds, meadows abloom with wildflowers of every shade.

The king and queen consulted with Dr. Ebon. "We want only happiness for her," they said. "And it makes her so sad to hear of things she cannot see."

"Then you must protect her," said Dr. Ebon. "Do not let her know what she is missing. Send out a proclamation throughout all the land that no one must tell the princess of the things they see on their flights. Furthermore, before she learns to read, you must gather all the books in the palace and lock them safely away from her sight. Reading of far-off places and seeing pictures of the wonders of the world will only serve to cause her pain."

This seemed extreme to the king and queen, but they would do anything to keep their beloved daughter happy. And so they issued a proclamation that no one should ever tell the princess of any place that existed beyond the palace walls. In addition, every book that hinted at wonders beyond the courtyard was collected and locked away in a room in the highest tower of the palace. A single door opened into the room, and this was locked tight and guarded from within by a trusted servant. The servant, an aged spectacled owl named Mrs. Bondadoso, was told that she must never, under any circumstances, open the door to anyone except the scullery maid who would bring her food three times a day, and to this charge she was completely faithful.

The only books that were left in the palace were cookbooks and instruction manuals on how to grow grain or how to season staves to be made into barrels. These the little princess came to love as she learned to read, for she knew of no other kind of book.

But her mother, the queen, missed the books that had been hidden away. She found herself longing to turn the pages, gaze at the illustrations, and read the words of her favorite volumes. So, privately, she conferred with Mrs. B., the guardian owl.

"When I desire entrance, I will come to the door and sing this song," said the queen.

Chick-a-ree, pip-it, pa-cheep, swee-swee
As grass to the meadow and wave to the sea
Chick-a-ree, pip-it, pa-cheep, swee-swee.

"You must not open the door unless you hear this song," she said. And so it was arranged.

In the meantime, Princess Sophia was growing more winsome every day, and her singing became more and more beautiful.

"Her voice rivals that of her mother, the queen," people would say. All who heard her were captivated.

But even more remarkable than her song was her gentle and loving spirit. She was kind and generous, good-natured and patient, wise beyond her years and infinitely compassionate. Birds from all over the kingdom flocked to the palace just to hear the little princess sing. But after sensing her goodness, they stayed to talk with her, to share with her their own particular heartaches.

As word of her benevolence spread, sad and broken birds of all kinds began to come to her, to hear her song, to share their stories, and to receive her sweet embrace. For though the little bird had only one good wing, she never failed to wrap both—one frail, one strong—around a visiting friend.

The princess was happy, but she still sometimes longed to fly—to soar with the other birds in the bright blue heavens.

One day Princess Sophia was hopping about the palace when she noticed a door she had never seen before. It was cracked open. With some effort, she pulled it wide enough to squeeze through. A long staircase wound upward as far as she could see. Curious, the little bird began hopping up the steps. Up, up, up she went.

The stairwell soon became dark and narrow, and she could hear the scurrying of mice in the walls. To give herself courage, the little bird began to sing. At last she reached the top. There, before her, stood an enormous oak door with neither handle nor lock. She pushed against it, but it did not budge. She tried knocking, but the door was so big and she so small that her little *rat-tat-tat* was like no sound at all.

The little bird was tired from her climb, so she sat to rest before starting the long trek back down the staircase. As she rested, she began to sing the song that her mother, the queen, always sang to her at bedtime.

Chick-a-ree, pip-it, pa-cheep, swee-swee
As grass to the meadow and wave to the sea

Chick-a-ree, pip-it, pa-cheep, swee-swee.

Suddenly the door swung open. A kindly plump owl stood there, looking as surprised as the little bird.

"Land's sake, Princess!" said the guardian owl. "I thought you were your mother!" Then, in wonderment: "You sound just like your mother."

The old owl tried to block the view of the room behind her, but the little bird hopped past.

"Books!" cried the princess. "Hundreds and hundreds of books!" She hopped about the room excitedly. It was filled from floor to ceiling with books of every size, shape, and color. She stopped in front of an enormous bookcase. With great effort, she pulled a book from a bottom shelf. Plopping down onto the floor, she drew it toward her and opened the cover. As she turned each page, she twittered with delight.

"I feel as though my withered wing has become strong and whole as I look at these pictures," she said, looking up at Mrs. B. "It's like I can fly—like I can soar right into other worlds, other places and times!"

Mrs. B., seeing the princess's joy, could not bring herself to scold or take the book away.

"But you must leave soon, Princess," she said, turning her head nervously in all directions. "We would both be in great trouble if you were discovered here."

"But why?" asked the princess. "What could be so wrong about reading these glorious books?"

"I don't know," said the owl. "But it is forbidden. I was told I must open the door for no one—except the maid who brings me food each day. And, on occasion, your mother."

"I would not want you to get in trouble," said the little bird. "I will leave now, but please, may I come back?"

"I don't know," said the owl nervously. "I have strict orders."

"Please," begged the little princess. "Just one more time? There are so many books left to explore, and they bring me such joy!"

"All right," said the softhearted owl. "Just one more time. But you must come early in the morning, for your mother comes only in the evenings, after you are asleep."

And so the next morning the little bird returned to the room of books. And the next. And the next. And always, when it was time to leave, she would beg to be able to come again.

"Just one more time," the kind Mrs. B. would say.

Those were joyful days for the little bird. Early each morning she would hop up the long stairwell to pore over the books, and for the rest of the day she would sing and listen to the stories of her many visitors, always giving them a kind word and a warm hug as they left.

Then one day, the queen woke early and decided to visit the vault of books while the rest of the palace slept. And there she discovered her beloved daughter, happily lost in a lavishly illustrated volume detailing the rivers of the world.

The queen was upset and called for the king and Dr. Ebon.

"You have disobeyed the orders of the king and queen," Dr. Ebon said to Mrs. B. "You must be punished."

"No, please!" cried the little bird. "It's my fault. She was only doing what I begged her to do. She was only allowing me some happiness. See how happy I am!"

Her parents looked at her, and they could see that it was true.

And so the books were carried back down and spread throughout the palace for all to enjoy. Often the little bird would share a favorite book with one of her visitors, and both would be cheered.

And so her days were spent singing, listening, sharing her books, and bestowing her hugs.

One day, the little princess noticed that her wing seemed stronger. She hopped to the center of the courtyard. Fluttering with all her might, she felt herself lift a few inches off the ground. Up . . . up . . . *crash*! She fell to the courtyard floor with a clatter. The king and queen came running. Seeing her in a heap upon the ground, they called for Dr. Ebon.

At first he was angry that they had not followed his orders to keep the withered wing bound.

"But look," said the little bird, dusting herself off. "I am not hurt. I am glad my parents did not bind my wing, for see what I can do because they did not." And she reached up with both wings and gave the doctor a warm hug. Tears began to run down the old doctor's face, for he had experienced little love in his life.

"Thank you," he said to the little bird. Then he spoke to the king and queen. "Forgive me," he said. "I thought I was doing the right thing to counsel you as I did. You see, Your Majesty," he said to the king, "before you were born, you had a brother. He was sickly, but I urged your parents to let him fly. He was not strong enough. He did not live. I have always held myself responsible. I was only trying to protect you and the princess."

"You are forgiven," said the little bird. "You only did what you thought best." And as she hugged him again, she felt a brief pulse of energy in her withered wing.

As the years passed, the princess continued to sing, and to listen, and to minister to others. And as she did, her shriveled wing grew gradually stronger.

When her aged parents passed on, Princess Sophia became Queen Sophia and reigned over Volaria in their stead. She ruled wisely and well and was greatly loved by all her subjects.

On the twentieth anniversary of her ascension to the throne, a great celebration was held. All who knew and loved Queen Sophia came to honor her. As she sat upon her throne, all the birds who had ever received comfort, counsel, and cheer from her approached, one by one, and knelt before her. With great tenderness, Queen Sophia touched each one lightly on the head with her feeble wing, bestowing on them her last blessing. As they continued to come, hundreds upon hundreds of them, a strange tingling moved throughout her body.

As the last bird reverently bowed and received the queen's blessing, then turned to join the throngs gathered in the courtyard, the queen felt a surge of wondrous warmth flow through her once-ruined wing. Rising to her full height, she slowly opened both wings to their full expanse. Then, with a great rushing sound, as though from the wings of angels, she lifted off from the earth, up, up, up, and soared away into the endless blue of the sky.

SHARLEE GLENN

Sharlee Glenn writes essays, short stories, poetry, middle-grade novels, and picture books. Recent publications include *Keeping Up with Roo* (Putnam), winner of the Dolly Gray Children's Literature Award, and *Just What Mama Needs* (Harcourt), which was featured on the Emmy Award-winning PBS children's show *Between the Lions*. Her next book, a non-fiction picture book entitled *Mary Did It Anyway: Mary Lemist Titcomb and America's First Bookmobile*, will be published by Abrams Books in 2016.

Sharlee lives in Pleasant Grove, Utah, with her husband and the youngest of their five children. Besides reading and writing, she loves hiking, yoga, listening to good music (especially when it's performed by her children), serving in her church, gabbing with friends, and watching BBC period dramas.

http://www.sharleeglenn.com/

ELI
(T-Cell Acute
Lymphoblastic Leukemia)

MEET ELI! On July 8, 2014, Eli was diagnosed with T-cell acute lymphoblastic leukemia. About a week prior, Eli complained of a sore on his tongue. His mother had also noticed that he did not have as much energy as normal and that he had complained of breathing difficulties a couple of times. Concerned, his mother took him to see the doctor.

The doctor ordered a chest X-ray, which revealed a mass of cells clustered by his thymus. The doctor immediately sent Eli and his mother to Primary Children's Hospital, where they spent the next two weeks. Not only will Eli have to undergo chemotherapy, but he will also need radiation treatment on his brain to fully eradicate his cancer.

Eli's loves all types of extreme sports, including motocross, monster trucks, skateboarding, and BMX. His dream is to soar high on his BMX bike, free of cancer and away from a hospital.

Eli Rides the Sky
Clint Johnson

The thirty best BMX Big Air riders in the world stood in a line at the foot of the tower. It stretched above them like a giant crane. Beneath the steel skeleton, all thirty riders in padded suits straddled their bikes. Some jumped up and down on shock absorbers strong enough to cushion an elephant. With helmets either on handlebars or beneath an arm, each rider looked at his competitors and smirked.

Each believed he was the best.

A boy, a foot too short and half too small, walked his bike to the end of the line. Thirty heads turned to look at the boy.

"Hey, kid," one rider said. "Did you lose your mom or something?"

"No," the boy said. "I'm just waiting to make my first jump."

The riders looked at each other in surprise. Then they laughed. They laughed long and hard and loud.

A rider with a long beard on his chin but no hair on his cheeks smirked at the boy. "What's your name, bitty bro? We can put it on your grave after you splat."

All the riders laughed again.

"Eli," the boy said. "And don't worry about me. I won't splat. I'll fly."

The bearded rider opened his mouth to speak again, but a shrill whine interrupted him. Louder than an ambulance roaring through the street, the whine sounded as a spark cut its way into the sky. High above, it exploded into streamers of hot white light. Soon after, a blue explosion followed, then red, then a combination of green and flashing silver. The noise sounded like giants heating popcorn.

As the fireworks burst above them, the bearded rider pointed at Eli. He mashed his hands together in a splat motion. Grinning, he showed Eli two dark holes where teeth were missing.

As the fireworks ended, the crowd roared and clapped. Thousands of people on Eli's left, and thousands of people on Eli's right, all stood and stomped and clapped their hands. "Jump!" they chanted. "Jump! Jump! Jump!"

The bearded rider looked into the sky, which was filled with a cloud that had not been there moments before. Smoke from the fireworks.

"I bet I can touch it," the bearded rider bragged.

"No way, Goat Boy," said a rider with a ring in his nose. "But I can!"

"No, I can," said another.

As every other rider argued that he and he alone could reach the cloud, Eli looked at the smoke filling the sky. He looked, and he studied, and he thought. "I can reach it," Eli said softly to himself. "I can fly."

The bearded rider heard him and snorted. "Have fun splatting, itty-bitty Eli. I'd ask for your bike, but it's too small for a real rider."

Eli looked at his bike, easily half the size as any other rider's. But it was just right for him, and that was all he cared about.

A voice so big and loud it seemed to come from the cloud itself roared to the X-Games crowd: "Ladies and gentlemen, welcome to the final event of the games and the greatest show above the earth! The BMX Big Air Final! Riders, up the ramp!"

Every rider put on his helmet, each decorated with a frightening image. Some showed skulls, some monsters with huge teeth, and some with mean-looking cars that spat fire from their tailpipes. Eli put on his helmet: simple black with a red stripe.

The line of riders rode up the tower. Up, and up, and up. The higher they rose, the less they spoke. They stared at the smoke in the sky in awe. As high as they climbed, the cloud had not grown any closer.

"I don't think I can reach that," one rider finally admitted.

Another nodded. "Give me an airplane, then maybe."

"I can do it," the bearded rider said again, but he didn't sound like he believed himself.

Eli stared along with the rest, but softly he said to himself, "I can reach it." This time no one laughed at him, because no one heard.

The first rider walked his bike to the edge of the ramp, which, from the top of the tower looked like a cliff. Shaking just a little, maybe from the wind, maybe from fear, he waited at the top. Then, in a moment of courage, he plunged.

Eli didn't even watch his trick. Instead, he stared up at the cloud.

Rider after rider followed, each one standing at the edge, shivering, then taking the plunge down the ramp. As points began to show on the huge scoreboard, causing the crowd to cheer or groan, the riders shook their heads. No one came anywhere near the cloud of smoke.

"It's not possible," the bearded rider finally admitted. Toeing his way to the cliff's edge, he pulled down his visor. "I won't even try."

"I will," Eli said. "I can fly."

"You can't fly," the rider snarled. "You aren't even brave enough to ride, not Big Air. Not once you're standing here." After taking a single big breath, he put his foot on his pedals and tipped himself over the edge.

It was now Eli's turn.

Calmly, little Eli rolled his little bike to edge of the biggest ramp in the world. He looked down. The ramp was as wide as a highway and fell nearly straight down. The surface was bright and slick and brown, like a basketball court or bowling alley. Only it plummeted down nearly a hundred feet, then curved into a ramp the size of a small mountain. Across a gap as wide as a canyon, the other side of the ramp rose into a straight lip for riders to perform their final trick.

Every rider who looked from the edge saw something frightening. Some feared

the gauge, which said two miles per hour. Then, smiling, he plunged down the ramp again, knowing he could fly higher.

CLINT JOHNSON

Clint Johnson is a writer and teacher of writing. In addition to his creative writing, he currently teaches developmental writing at Salt Lake Community College and is a contributing writer for ESPN's TrueHoop Utah Jazz site, Salt City Hoops.

http://ClintJohnsonWrites.com

RAE

(Diffuse Intrinsic
Pontine Giloma or DIPG)

Meet Rae! Rae is a beautiful, fun little girl with a personality that is completely bubbling over. She has beaten the odds and is an absolute inspiration. Only five percent of people diagnosed with the type of brain cancer she has survive more than a year. She has passed that benchmark and, as of this writing, is still going strong.

She is a perfect example of never giving up, that hope should never be lost. Every day she is alive is another huge blessing to her family. I recently discovered that Rae's tumor has actually decreased in size, which is a miracle. We hope it will keep on getting smaller!

Rae's dream is to become a princess, and I have no doubt that she will be one someday. For now I hope she can look at her images and dream away. May we all recognize how special we are every time we look in the mirror.

THE PRINCESS IN THE MIRROR
Linda Gerber

ONCE UPON A TIME, IN A FARAWAY KINGDOM, lived a kind king and his very gentle queen. The king, riding through the woods one day, came across an old woman stranded in the middle of a swift-moving stream. He leaped from his horse and waded into the current to carry the woman to safety.

"There now, Grandmother," he soothed as he wrapped her in his kingly cloak. "What an ordeal you've been through. Come, let me take you to the palace, where you may rest."

The queen, seeing her husband return home with a shivering old woman on his horse, ran to the courtyard to meet them. "Dear lady," she fussed, "your skin is blue with cold. Quick, let us warm you by the fire."

In the palace parlor, the queen settled the old woman onto her own soft chair and exchanged the woman's sodden shoes for slippers lined with fur. She summoned her lady-in-waiting to find a dry frock the woman could wear.

"Thank you, dear," said the woman, "but that won't be necessary. You two have already proven yourselves to be both gentle and kind. Allow me to introduce myself. I am Felicia, your fairy grandmother. I would like to reward your kindness with a gift."

"Grandmother?" asked the queen.

"Gift?" asked the king.

Felicia smiled a crinkly smile. She flicked her wrist and a sparkly—though somewhat bent—magic wand appeared. Her rags fell away to reveal a rather wrinkled but nonetheless splendid taffeta gown. Similarly creased but beautiful diaphanous wings sprouted from her stooped shoulders. Her silver hair arranged itself into a smart French twist. "A gift," she repeated. "For you, or for your child."

"But . . . we have no child," said the queen.

"Not yet," said Felicia. And with that, she was gone.

The next spring, the queen gave birth to a tiny baby girl. The princess was a beautiful child, golden, like a ray of sunshine.

"We shall call her Rae," said the king.

"A lovely name," said Felicia.

"Oh!" cried the queen. "Fairy Grandmother! I didn't hear you come in."

"I'm quiet that way," said Felicia. She crossed to the silk-draped bassinet and peered in. "Hello, sweetling. My, you are precious."

The king leaned closer. The queen held her breath. Their child was about to receive a fairy gift.

Indeed, Felicia pulled out her bent magic wand, but she didn't conjure anything with it. Instead, she sang to Princess Rae, beating out the tempo as if she held a conductor's baton.

"Beauty is what beauty sees,
Strength inside is what will be,
Reflection is your kindest friend,
To give you hope around the bend."

Before the king and queen could ask what that meant, the fairy grandmother disappeared in a poof of silver dust and sparkles. In her place stood a tall mirror in a simple black frame.

"What is that?" asked the king.

"The gift," guessed the queen. "It's very plain. Do you suppose it's magic?"

The king drew back. "Oh, no. No magic mirrors. You saw what happened a few kingdoms over with that witch queen and the pale princess. Out it goes."

"No!" cried the queen. "One does not toss out a fairy gift. It's bad form and bad luck."

"Fine," conceded the king. "We'll put it in the dungeon."

So into the dungeon it went, but the next time the king and queen entered Princess Rae's bedchamber, there the mirror stood.

"The attic," suggested the queen.

And so the mirror was stowed in the deepest shadows of the attic, behind four large crates of outdated heraldry. But, as before, by the time the king and queen returned to the princess's side, there was the mirror, leaning casually against the wall.

"May as well let it stay," said the queen.

"Keep a close eye on it," warned the king.

But as these things go, days and weeks and months passed without incident, and soon the mystery of the mirror was forgotten.

Meanwhile, Rae grew from a beautiful baby into an adorable toddler, and from an adorable toddler into a perfect princess. She was kind like her father and gentle like her mother. Her parents' only concern was that, although Princess Rae charmed the knights and amused the ladies-in-waiting, she had no friends her age to play with in the palace. Instead, she spent what they considered to be an unprincessly amount of time alone in her room.

"We should arrange a royal playdate," suggested the king, "so she can meet people."

"We should throw a princess party," suggested the queen, "so she can make friends."

"But I have a friend," said Rae.

"You do?" asked the queen.

"Who?" asked the king.

Rae smiled. "The princess in the mirror."

The king and queen exchanged worried glances. Was their poor daughter so lonely she was keeping company with her own reflection? It was all well and fine when she'd been a baby, gurgling and giggling in front of the mirror for hours on end, but recently they'd heard her talking to the air, carrying on complete conversations with herself.

"An imaginary friend," whispered the queen.

"I'm not so sure," whispered the king. "This is the fairy mirror that couldn't stay put."

The queen grew pale. "Rae, darling," she said. "I would like to meet your friend."

The king and queen followed Rae to her royal bedchamber, worry weighing their every step. But when Rae proudly showed them her mirror, all the king and queen saw was their own darling daughter reflected in the glass. No alarming green-tinted masks. No magic.

"No harm," said the king.

"No alarm," said the queen.

They left Rae with her mirror and gently pulled the door closed behind them.

"What was that all about?" asked the princess in the mirror.

Rae shrugged. "Couldn't tell you," she said. "One never knows with grown-ups."

"Your move," said the princess.

Rae settled into her chair and considered the chessboard before the mirror. She cautiously moved a piece. "Check," she said.

"Ha, ha!" crowed the princess in the mirror. "You underestimated my pawn!" She moved the piece on her reflected board. "Checkmate."

Another year came and went. Palace procedures and kingdom commitments overtook the king and queen, and the mirror was forgotten once again.

Rae began her princess training. Her days were soon filled with a parade of tutors, music maestros, archery instructors, and one very finicky manners mistress. Each day, Rae shared with the princess in the mirror all the things that she had learned.

"We start dance instruction today," Rae said sulkily one morning. "I'd much rather take up something practical. Like fencing, for instance."

"Well, fencing is rather like a dance," said the princess. "Just pretend you have a foil in your hand, like so." She whirled about with an imaginary weapon. "*Balestra! Lunge!*"

Rae giggled and followed the footing. "*Passe arriere!*"

"Very good," cried the dance instructor, who just happened to be passing by the room. "Pleased to see you are practicing. Shall we continue in the studio?"

Rae bobbed a quick curtsey and grabbed her dance slippers. "Thank you," she whispered to the princess in the mirror. "You saved me."

"You saved yourself," the princess whispered back.

Princess Rae and her mirror companion continued to spend countless hours together. They played together, studied together, and when a new, strict riding master took over in the stables, they complained together.

"He doesn't think I can ride the Turk," Rae pouted. "Says I'm too timid for such a spirited horse." She slouched in her chair. "I don't know. Maybe he's right."

"Humph," said the princess in the mirror. "We shall see about that." She ran to her own stables, pausing at the door to listen. "Come on," she said softly and tiptoed inside.

Rae leaned closer to the glass to watch and held her nose because the barn smelled of unmucked stalls. "Careful," she whispered nasally.

The princess in the mirror just smiled. She pulled a shiny, red apple from her pocket and waltzed to the Turk's stall. "Here you are, boy," she cooed. "I have a treat for you."

The horse whinnied happily and lipped the apple from the princess's hand.

He munched loudly for a moment and then nuzzled her for more. She stroked his bristly-silky nose. "Next time," she promised and threw Rae a meaningful glance.

The following afternoon, Princess Rae was sure to bring an apple to her riding lessons. "I'd like to ride the Turk, please," she said sweetly.

"Nazar?" the riding master scoffed. "Certainly not, Princess. He's cunning as a unicorn and twice as wild. He'd throw you off inside a royal minute."

"He *likes* me," Rae said and marched right up to the Turk's stall. "Don't you, boy?" She slipped the sugar from her pocket and fed it to Nazar, then led the horse confidently to the riding arena.

To her riding master's astonishment, Rae rode the horse without incident for her entire lesson.

"How did it go?" asked the princess in the mirror when Rae returned to her room.

"Perfect," said Rae. "Thank you for the apple idea. I couldn't have done it without you."

"Sure you could," said the princess in the mirror.

More time passed. Spring turned into summer, and summer into fall. Snow fell and melted away again. And then one day, Rae sensed a change in the air that had nothing to do with the seasons.

"What is it, Father?" she asked.

"Not now, my dear," said the king.

"What's wrong, Mother?" Rae asked.

"Don't worry, darling," said the queen.

But Rae did worry. She watched through the keyhole as the king assembled his advisors in the council hall and gathered his bravest knights. The men stood in fretful circles, murmuring in tones too low for Rae to hear.

"Sweetheart," chided the queen, "come away from there. Princesses do not eaves-drop."

"They do when no one will tell them what's going on," Rae grumbled.

"Now, now," the queen said gently. "Why don't you work on your—" Her words were cut off by a ruckus erupting on the other side of the council hall door. Rae returned to her keyhole.

"Dragons in the kingdom!" shouted the viceroy.

"They have sealed the southern border!" bellowed the chaplain.

"Let us fight!" cried the knights.

The king begged for calm. "Perhaps they mean no harm," he said. "If we could just reason with them—"

"There is no reasoning with dragons," countered the councilors. "They would fry us where we stand."

"Our horses won't go near them," confirmed the knights. "And it's much too dangerous to approach on foot. The armor clanks, you see."

"But . . . diplomacy," sputtered the king.

Princess Rae backed away from the door. She had to help her father and her kingdom. But what could one small princess do? She ran straight to her room to ask the princess in the mirror. As she opened the door, however, she heard a horrible crash.

"Oh, Highness!" the chambermaid cried. "Forgive me. I was polishing your mirror and it fell." Sure enough, shards of glass lay at her feet, along with a mangled frame.

Anger and sadness and fear jumbled together and squeezed Rae's chest like a too-tight corset. It wasn't easy, but she tried to be gentle and kind. "Nothing to forgive," she said. "It was an accident."

The maid curtsied contritely and scurried off to find a broom. Alone in her bedchamber, Rae sank to the floor amid the slivers of mirror and sobbed.

"Oh, dear. This won't do," said Felicia.

"Fairy Grandmother!" cried Rae.

"Now what's all this fuss about?" Felicia asked. "I thought you were off to fight the dragons."

Rae shook her head. Her shoulders drooped in defeat. "I can't," she said. "The princess in the mirror is gone."

"But my dear," Felicia said gently, "you *are* the princess in the mirror. She is but a reflection of who you truly are"—she tapped her finger over her heart—"in here. So tell me, Princess, what would your mirror-self do?"

Rae sniffled. She wiped her eyes. "She . . . she would face the dragons and save her kingdom."

"Good show," said Felicia as she faded away. "Now get to work!"

Rae stood and dusted herself off. She was small like a pawn, and not threatening like a knight. Perhaps she could approach the dragons without getting fried and convince them to go home. She grabbed her traveling cloak, and a fencing foil for good measure, and ran down the turret stairs before she could change her mind.

The riding master saw Rae dash to the stables. "Princess!" he called. "No lesson today!"

But Rae pretended not to hear him and rushed to open Nazar's stall. She jumped onto the horse's back and grabbed handfuls of his mane so she wouldn't fall off. They bolted past the riding master, clattered over the drawbridge, and galloped straight into the woods.

Near the border road, Rae smelled the dragons' terrible brimstone breath. Her stomach twisted with fear. They must be close. She hid Nazar behind a tree and slid down from his back.

"Stay here until I come for you," she whispered.

Rae pushed through the brambles and branches until she spied a thunder of fierce-looking dragons stomping across the road. At the sight of them, Rae shrank back and hid behind a bush, trembling.

But then she thought of her mother and father. She thought of her kingdom. She thought of the princess in the mirror. She must be brave, for them.

Peeking through the leaves, Rae watched the dragons march in a huge, lumbering circle, around and around and around again. Sunlight shimmered across their scales with every step. The movement was mesmerizing. Rae was so drawn to the light that before she could stop herself, she stepped out from her hiding place.

One of dragons turned its head toward her, eyes narrowing into angry yellow slits. A jolt of fear shot through Rae and broke the spell. She ducked back into the bush and shielded her eyes from the light.

It didn't take her long to realize that the dragons were just as captivated by the flashes of gold and green as she had been. Indeed, each dazed dragon followed the dazzle of the dragon in front of it, one after the other, like one big turning wheel. The dragons weren't invading or blocking the trade route; they were spellbound by the sparkles.

That gave Rae an idea. She drew a deep breath for courage, then stood and waved her fencing foil above her head. Sunlight glinted along the blade. She danced as she'd done in her room with the princess in the mirror. The dragons stopped their parade.

"That's it," Rae said. "Now we just need to turn you homeward."

She wasn't sure where their home was exactly, but she guessed it must be back down the road somewhere. Whirling and twirling with her foil, Rae led the dragons away from the kingdom's border. She danced until her arms grew heavy and her slippers split. Then, when the dragons were pointed in the right direction, she ducked aside and let them follow their own flashing scales beyond the horizon and out of sight.

Kicking off her ruined slippers, Rae limped back to where she had left Nazar. Her heart dropped right to the dusty road when she saw the riding master waiting for her, holding the horse's reins. She was going to be in such trouble! But to her surprise, instead of lecturing her, the riding master bowed when Rae approached.

"My lady," he said. "That was amazing."

Back at the palace, the knights knelt and the councilors cheered.

"Good show," said the king.

"Bravely done," said the queen.

"Well earned," said Felicia. For next to the fairy grandmother stood Rae's magic mirror. The princess inside waved delightedly.

"You fixed it!" cried Rae. "She's back!"

Felicia smiled. "Yes, well, one's true self cannot rightly go away, can it?"

"Thank you, Fairy Grandmother," Rae said.

"Ah, it was nothing," Felicia said, smoothing her silver coif. "Besides, you may need a friend when your little brother becomes a bother."

"But . . . I don't have a little brother," said Rae.

"Not yet," said Felicia with her twinkly smile. "Not yet."

LINDA GERBER

Linda should have been born a princess. Instead, she grew up in a college town in the shadows of the Wasatch Mountains in Utah, where she avoided her homework by making up stories and daydreaming about faraway kingdoms. Currently, she lives in Japan, still dreaming, and spinning stories into books.

http://www.lindagerber.com/

ELLIE
(Undifferentiated
Sarcoma of the Kidney)

MEET ELLIE! Ellie was diagnosed with stage 2 undifferentiated sarcoma of the kidney in the middle of 2013. It is a really rare type of cancer, especially in children. She is currently in remission and is back at school and having somewhat of a normal life. For the next five years, though, she will be closely monitored, and we all hope relapse will not be an issue.

Ellie's dream is to be a baker. I didn't want her to be just any baker—I wanted her to be an amazing baker who could do things that seem impossible. I think that the fight against cancer can feel like a losing battle sometimes, so I want anyone who looks at this image to believe that anything is possible, even overcoming cancer!

Ellie the Baker
Adam Glendon Sidwell

Grandma was sick. Mom told Ellie after school that Grandma had fallen and was going to be in the hospital for two days.

Ellie didn't understand how serious the words "critical" or "concussion" were in a medical sense. They sounded bad, but the doctors would fix it, right?

On the day Grandma came home from the hospital, Ellie flung open the kitchen screen door and scrambled down the back steps, jogging across the back lawn and into the woods that grew between her backyard and Grandma's house.

It did not take long for her to dart down the winding, jagged path under the crisscrossing shadows of trees and reach the other side of the wood. She barely knocked on Grandma's back door—she never needed to; it was always unlocked—before letting herself in.

"Ellie?" said a weak voice from Grandma's room.

Ellie poured a glass of cool water, placed a napkin under it, and took it to Grandma's room.

Ellie did not recognize the person in the big bed at first. The woman propped up on pillows was paler and frailer than Grandma had ever been. Her eyes were glassy. "Ellie?" she said again.

Ellie recognized the voice. It was her grandma, only she sounded as if her voice was calling from far away.

Grandma turned her head and smiled. "Now there's a pretty sight," she said, her breathing strained.

"Hello, Grandma," said Ellie, her voice shaky. She held back her tears. Grandma had always been as constant as summertime or Christmas. Ellie did not know her grandma could change. She wasn't sure what to say. "How . . . how are you feeling?" Ellie handed her the water.

"I'm in good shape for the shape I'm in," said Grandma. She took a sip of water, then spooned a thick, yellow paste into her mouth. She grimaced.

"If only I had something sweet enough, I think I'd live forever," Grandma said. This time her eyes twinkled. It was a sparkle that must have come from deep inside, because it glistened like a dewdrop at dawn, and that meant Grandma had spoken the truth.

A sudden thrill rose inside Ellie, and she seized hold of it. It was hope.

She turned from the room and rushed into the kitchen, throwing open the cupboard above the oven where she knew the old, red, leather-bound book of Grandma's handwritten recipes was hidden. The cover was cracked, and the loose sheets of paper were yellow with age. Grandma's personal recipe book was famous. Ellie had heard Mom or the aunties or any number of her cousins talk about it with reverence and awe at Christmastime or during summer camping trips when the scattered lines of Grandma's descendants were gathered together.

Ellie felt a twinge of guilt as she hugged the book to her chest and ran from Grandma's house into the woods. "You know how many people have tried to get their hands on that book?" one of her aunts had said last Fourth of July. Black crows flapped and cawed back and forth as they landed in thick, heavy layers on the tree branches above her. They seemed to speak to each other, as if planning their nighttime activities. Ellie wondered if they were mentioning her and doubled her pace.

When she was finally clear of the trees, and the back door to her own house was shut tight behind her, she opened the recipe book in the kitchen. The handwritten, cursive recipes were all written in pencil with Grandma's long, looping letters. Ellie had never baked before, and she did not know sifting from folding, or baking powder from baking soda, but Grandma had said what she'd said, and in that there was hope.

With Mom's help, Ellie baked her first cake. It sagged in the middle where the batter was still soggy, and there were bits of sharp eggshell that she had not been able to pick out mixed in. She shoveled the entire mess into the trash can and cried. She wanted to make Grandma something sweet. She *needed* to do this.

The second cake was also a struggle. But the third cake was an improvement. By the fourth day, Ellie had baked a round vanilla cake with blue frosting that caused Mom to nod her head in approval. Ellie sealed the cake in a plastic container and ran through the shadows in the woods, the crows fluttering above her, to Grandma's house.

"Grandma, I made this for you, so you'll get better," said Ellie. She held out a slice of cake on a plate. Ellie was hopeful for a moment. She had created something sweet, and she felt the thrill that came with it.

Grandma propped herself up in bed, then slowly took a bite, sliding the fork from her mouth smoothly. Her eyes cleared, and she stared into Ellie's face like she was reading her.

Ellie's hope turned to anxiety. Grandma might recognize her own recipe. Would she know Ellie had stolen her prized book? No one in all their family had ever done that. It was too late for confessions now.

Grandma did not accuse her. Instead, she was thoughtful for a long moment.

"I wonder what lemon-flavored might taste like," she finally said. Her lips did not show a hint of a smile, nor did her gaze leave Ellie's face.

Ellie's heart sank. Did Grandma not like the cake? Ellie studied the old woman's face. There was no hint hidden in the wrinkles there.

Ellie ran from Grandma's room and back through the woods, the cake clutched in both arms. Tears burst from her eyes. In all her life, she'd never known Grandma to do anything but praise her: "Oh, my, what an artistic masterpiece," or "Don't you look like a picture-perfect sweetheart." Nothing but approval had ever escaped Grandma's lips.

The crows seemed to laugh at her as she ran past.

It was a whole day before she began work on the lemon cake. By now she didn't need Mom's help. Ellie understood what sifting and folding meant and that she should mix the dry ingredients first before adding the wet ones. She knew how to crack eggs without losing track of the shells. She knew how to make the frosting soft but firm.

Before she put the cake into the oven, she overheard the next-door neighbor in the living room talking to Mom. Her back was to the kitchen.

"This is very good," the neighbor said. She was holding a fork in one hand with a slice of Ellie's vanilla cake with blue frosting on a plate in the other. She took another bite. "I mean *really* good," she said, her mouth full of cake. "Who made this?"

The neighbor didn't know Ellie was listening. Ellie felt her chest swell. She had made that.

She pushed the lemon cake batter into the oven.

"Hmm," said Grandma as she slid the fork from her mouth later that afternoon. She chewed slowly while Ellie searched for signs of approval in Grandma's face. Again her face was a mask. "I wonder what German chocolate might taste like."

Again Ellie ran through the woods under the gathering crows with her cake clutched under her arms. She shoved the cake onto the kitchen counter and cried. Why didn't her grandma like the cakes?

The next morning, Ellie heard a knock on the door. It was the neighbor again, plus two more women from down the street. "Is your mother home?" she asked.

Ellie let them in and slipped away into the kitchen.

Mom met them in the living room, where the women spoke in low voices. Mom came into the kitchen where Ellie hid. She seemed puzzled. "They want cake," she said. She reached for the lemon cake and cut three slices.

And so it went, day after day. German chocolate, carrot cake, red velvet—all taken from Grandma's treasured book of handwritten recipes. But it wasn't just cakes anymore. Ellie made cupcakes and tarts and cookies, too. All layered with thick frosting in icy blue or soft white, with purple roses or green vines intertwined across the tops. The kitchen was a warm and colorful rainbow—chocolate cakes on the countertop, sugar cookies in the oven, slices of banana cake stacked in the corner, even donuts piled high on top the refrigerator.

Ellie practically had to balance stacks of cupcakes in one hand while rainbow-layered cakes teetered on top a spoon in the other hand just to get around the kitchen.

And, oh, the smells that came from the kitchen!

Each day Ellie tried to find that sweet something that would cure Grandma's pains. Each day, more people came, some of them friends, most of them strangers, asking for a bite of the wonder that were Ellie's cakes.

The taste-seekers came alone or in pairs at first, asking shyly for a taste, mentioning that they'd heard from so-and-so down the street just how good the cakes were and that they'd be willing to pay for the treats.

Mom set up a makeshift storefront in the garage with a sign and a cashbox, and the people kept coming. None of that made a difference to Ellie. She kept on baking. Her fame spread.

And every day, Grandma asked for a new flavor, and Ellie ran back through the woods to start again. But it was different now. Ellie did not seek Grandma's approval so much as her satisfaction.

Then one day, Grandma made a new request. "I wonder, Ellie, what a masterpiece might taste like?" She closed her eyes as if to go to sleep.

Ellie rushed back home, the cake in one hand, the heavy recipe book clutched in the other. The woods seemed darker that day, and Ellie, in her haste, did not see the protruding root. It caught her foot, and she fell. The cake tumbled out, and the book smashed to the ground, scattering the pages like leaves.

The crows fell like black stones, flapping and cawing, their beaks stabbing down onto both the cake and the pages of the book, scattering the recipes, tearing at the soft sponge and ripping everything to pieces. They clawed and bit, murderous and dark and furious.

In moments they were gone. There was nothing left of the treasure trove of hand-written recipes except for shreds of paper smeared in cake. The recipes were gone.

Ellie pushed herself up to her knees and sobbed. Her elbows were scraped, and her lip was bleeding. It was nothing compared to the pain she felt at losing the book. Now Ellie would have to tell Grandma not only that she'd stolen the book but that it was never coming back.

"Go away!" Ellie screamed at the crows. "Go away!" She threw the cake platter at them, scattering them so they took flight and disappeared above the trees.

She picked herself up and limped home.

For three days Ellie did not dare set foot in the kitchen. The aromas of all her former cakes haunted her—all smells from recipes written by Grandma's hand. All creations from the book. All products of Grandma's wisdom and her lifetime of experience. How could she make a cake without instructions from the book that had held them all? Ellie couldn't create something from nothing.

Grandma had requested a masterpiece. Ellie felt helpless.

"Which one is your favorite?" asked a stranger who stopped by with the rest of the crowds a day later. It was the first time someone had asked Ellie's opinion. She didn't know.

"I like the frosting on this one," she whispered, pointing to a thick chocolate double-layered cake with fudge frosting. "And this one's texture," she said, pointing to a dense strawberry cake. "And this one's got so many layers," she said, pointing to a very tall coconut-flavored cake.

"If you could make any cake, what would it be?" asked the man. It was a strange question. Ellie had never invented a cake. She only had followed instructions. But this man was asking *her*.

She turned back to the kitchen and donned her baker's hat. She had no recipe. But by now she knew the basic ingredients by heart. She knew how the sugar would blend with the butter into a creamy mixture. She knew how many eggs to add to give her the consistency she needed. She set aside the right amount of vanilla and baking powder and flour. She mixed the ingredients together, and finally, as if by instinct, she set the oven to 350 degrees. She could feel what was right. There was no invisible hand guiding hers. This was something Ellie *knew*.

When the cake was finished and Ellie opened the oven, the aroma filled the whole kitchen. She let the cake cool, then she frosted it with her own mixture of spicy fudge frosting. Then it was complete.

She sealed it in a cake box, removed her baker's hat, and then carefully hiked across the woods to Grandma's house.

Grandma was waiting for her. She was sitting at her kitchen table. Ellie opened the cake box. Grandma cocked one eyebrow as Ellie cut her a slice.

Grandma took a bite, wrapping her mouth around the dark morsel. Her eyes grew wide. "Fudge, with dense chocolate sponge, and . . . blueberries . . . wrapped in cream. And spices." She took another bite. "This is new," she said, wagging her fork at the slice. "This was never in my book of recipes."

Of course Grandma knew where all those cakes had come from. Ellie started to cry. "Oh, Grandma, I'm so sorry. You're famous treasure book of recipes . . . I took it, and now it's gone."

Grandma opened her arms, and Ellie nestled into her embrace, sobbing into her grandma's shoulder.

When she was done, Grandma held her at arm's length. "The book is gone, but those recipes are in here," she said, tapping Ellie on the chest. "It's a much safer place to keep them." She winked. "It's one way to live forever."

Grandma took a leather-bound book from underneath the table. Ellie opened it. The lined pages were empty.

"You are a baker now, Ellie. Fill a new book," said Grandma. She gave the book to Ellie.

And Ellie did.

ADAM GLENDON SIDWELL

In between writing books, Adam uses the power of computers to make monsters, robots, and zombies come to life for blockbuster movies, including *Pirates of the Caribbean, King Kong, Pacific Rim, Transformers,* and *Tron.* After spending countless hours in front of a keyboard meticulously adjusting tentacles, calibrating hydraulics, and brushing monkey fur, he is delighted at the prospect of modifying his creations with the flick of a few deftly placed adjectives.

Adam wrote every single word in the Evertaster series, the picture book *Fetch,* and the novel *Chum.* He once showed a famous movie star where the bathroom was.

http://www.evertaster.com/

TRISTAN
(Ewing's Sarcoma)

MEET TRISTAN! Tristan was diagnosed with a very aggressive form of bone cancer. In order to stop the cancer from spreading, Tristan's right leg was amputated just below the knee. Prior to his cancer, Tristan loved playing sports and was very athletic. Despite losing his leg, nothing has changed. Tristan is every bit as athletic as he was before, only now he has a cool metal prosthetic.

The fact that he lost his right leg to cancer has not stopped him from dreaming big!

He wants to play for the University of Utah and then play professional football for the San Francisco 49ers. He has a lot of work ahead of him to make that dream happen, but for now I plan to give him something to look forward to!

TRISTAN'S TOUCHDOWNS
Frank L. Cole

THE REFEREE'S WHISTLE WAS LIKE A GIANT VACUUM sucking the air straight out of the stadium. The Cosmo Cougars had just scored another touchdown, and the Bay Herriman fans dropped their posters and let out a sigh of disappointment.

Sitting on the sidelines with his helmet in his lap, Tristan Chidester glanced up at the scoreboard and shook his head. It was 21–3 with three minutes to go in the game. The Bombers' hopes of a state championship had ended with that last Cosmo touchdown.

"We gave it our best shot," Tristan heard their coach say.

"C'mon, Tristan," said Tanner, Tristan's older brother, "you're going in."

Tanner played defense and had done his part to keep the game close. But the Cosmo Cougars were just too good.

"They got lucky," Tristan muttered.

"I don't know," Tanner said. "They sacked Colin seven times!"

"Yeah, I was watching the same game."

Tristan didn't always get to play, and when he did it was mostly on special teams. Though he tried his best not to complain, his dream was to play quarterback, and watching his teammates take the field while he sat on the sidelines was frustrating at times.

Standing from the bench, Tristan fastened the chin strap of his helmet and hiked his sock up over his prosthetic leg. The prosthetic was custom-made with a gold lightning bolt painted on the side.

"Fullback," Coach announced to Tristan, patting him on the shoulder.

"Okay." Tristan trotted a few steps onto the field but hesitated. Fullback? There was only three minutes left of the season, and he didn't want to spend that time blocking for someone else. Gritting his teeth, Tristan turned to face his coach.

"Can I play quarterback?" he asked hopefully.

Coach frowned. "Sorry, that's Colin's position. It's his ball."

Tristan considered protesting, but Colin was his friend and deserved to be quarterback.

"He can have it," Colin said, moving up next to Coach. "I don't need to be QB for this play."

Coach Jim seemed on the verge of shouting at the senior for challenging his decision, but instead he merely itched his nose. "Fine. Colin, you'll play fullback. Tristan, keep it simple. No passing plays. We don't want the score to get out of hand."

"You didn't have to do that," Tristan said to Colin as they trotted onto the field.

Colin grinned mischievously. "Whatever, dude!" He handed Tristan the wristband with the team's playbook, and Tristan slipped it over his forearm. "Did you see what those guys did to me? Seven sacks! I don't want to throw against them anymore."

Tristan eyed the Cougar defense stepping up to the line. They were huge, and he knew they intended to smear as many Bomber players as they could before the final whistle sounded.

"What's the play, Colin?" one of Tristan's teammates asked when the two boys joined the huddle. It was Joe, the left tackle.

"Tristan's got the ball. Ask him," Colin answered.

"Right on!" said Michael, one of the wide receivers and Tristan's best friend. "It's about time."

Several hands smacked Tristan's helmet, and he felt his skin prickle with excitement. This was the moment he'd been waiting for since the surgery. The moment to prove the doubters wrong.

"What do you want to do?" Joe asked.

Tristan looked up at the scoreboard and smiled. "I want to win."

Most of the boys in the huddle started laughing as Tristan took a knee and flipped through the playbook. "We're running *Red Turkey*. Michael, I'm going to hit you in the corner."

Joe smirked. "*Red Turkey*? That's not in the playbook. You're making that up."

"I know *Red Turkey*," Michael said. He turned to Joe. "It always worked when Tristan called it in rec league." A few of the others players nodded in agreement. "Coach isn't going to like it."

Tristan shrugged. "We need a touchdown."

"Don't you know what the score is?" Joe pointed to the far end of the field. "You're joking, right?"

Tristan grabbed Joe by the face mask and pulled it within an inch of his own. "Do I look like I'm joking?" He narrowed his eyes but then gave Joe's helmet a friendly pat. "They're not expecting anything like this. Trust me. All right, boys, gobble, gobble."

Tristan stood behind Marcus, the center. Crowding the line, several Cosmo players were actually growling as they readied to attack. It would be a blitz, no doubt about it, but that was exactly what Tristan was counting on.

Dropping back, Tristan yelled, "Hike!" and immediately moved to avoid a Cosmo player who burst through the line and dove for his legs. He pulled his arm back and launched the ball just as a wall of players crashed into him. Collapsing beneath the Cosmo defense, Tristan watched his spiral soar down the field and into Michael's outstretched hands. There were no other players around, and Michael easily ran the ball into the end zone for a touchdown. The crowd of Bomber fans erupted.

"What was that?" Coach thumbed through his playbook, looking for an explanation.

After a successful kick, the lights on the board showcased the new score: 21–10, with two and a half minutes left.

"Are you insane?" Tanner asked Tristan after he'd jogged off the field.

"That was *Red Turkey*!"

"You have to get me the ball back," Tristan said.

Tanner raised an eyebrow. "How am I going to do that?"

Tristan winked. "You could try *Opening the Barn Door*. Remember that play?"

Tanner rolled his eyes. "This isn't rec league. If you upset Coach, he won't let either one of us on the team next season."

A hand snagged Tristan's jersey, spinning him around. "What was that?" Coach Jim demanded.

"Sorry, sir, I didn't know what else to do. Those guys are fast." He looked at the ground, trying to keep from smiling.

"Well, it was an amazing throw." As Coach Jim turned to instruct the defense, Michael leaped onto Tristan's back.

"Best pass of the year!" Michael cheered. "When I saw those guys on top of you, I thought you were dead."

"It felt like I was dead. They're heavy." Tristan snagged a water bottle and took a swig.

"I don't even care if we lose. That play made them look stupid."

"We're not losing this game."

"Yeah, I know, we just have to believe." Michael mockingly twirled his finger. "But in case you've forgotten, we also have to get our offense back on the field."

"I think we're about to."

Tristan focused on the field as Bay Herriman kicked the ball. Catching it just inside the ten-yard line, a Cosmo player took off in a sprint. He raced past the Bombers with ease, looking as though he would go all the way, with only Tanner remaining at midfield. The player hesitated, but then sidestepped around Tanner, who seemed frozen in place. Coach Jim slammed his clipboard on the ground and shook his fist. How could Tanner, a top-notch defender, just stand there like a statue?

Then, as the Cosmo player headed for yet another touchdown, Tanner reacted, swiping out and knocking the ball free.

"Fumble!" the Cougars screamed on the field.

"Fumble!" the Bombers shouted from the sidelines.

"*Barn Door!*" Tristan slapped Michael in the chest as they watched Tanner scoop up the loose football. He was tackled shortly after, but the damage had been done. Bay Herriman was facing the end zone with ninety seconds left to play.

Once again the offense huddled together with Tristan in the middle.

"What now?" Michael asked eagerly.

"They're probably expecting a pass, so let's keep them guessing." Tristan didn't even look at the playbook. If they were going to pull this off, they would have to do it his way.

"Running the ball is going to waste time," Joe said.

"Not if we do *Tippy Toes*." Tristan divvied out instructions.

"These are seriously the dumbest play names I've ever heard," Joe grumbled.

"But they work." Tristan jabbed his finger at Joe. "Just make sure you keep them away from me."

Directly after the snap, Tristan faked the handoff to Carlos, the running back, and several Cougars chased after him before realizing he didn't have the ball. Tristan dashed through a hole in the line, pumping his legs as fast as he could. But there were too many players standing in the way, and he knew they would tackle him if he kept running.

Turning sharply, Tristan jogged toward the sideline. The Cougars slowed down as well, expecting the whistle to blow announcing the end of the play. But instead of stepping out of bounds, Tristan made his move. While toeing the imaginary tightrope of the sideline, he blurred past the defense and sprinted into the end zone.

Tristan spiked the ball as his teammates plowed him over like he was a tackling dummy. The score was now 21–17 with thirty seconds to go. The Cougars no longer looked confident of the win.

"I know that's not one of my plays," Coach said. Tristan was worried he'd be angry and so was surprised when the coach suddenly pulled him into a massive bear hug. "Unbelievable! You don't happen to have any ideas for an onside kick, do you?"

After thinking for a moment, Tristan glanced down with a grin. "I was hoping you'd ask."

The kickoff unit lined up for the onside kick, and to everyone's shock, Tristan stood behind the football. Several parents shouted from the stands, demanding to know why Phil, the usual placekicker, wasn't on the field.

Holding up his hand, Tristan nodded to his coach before booting the ball high into the air. It soared to the right, barely passing the ten-yard marker.

The Cougars scrambled, trying to snatch the ball before Bay Herriman could get there. The fans held their breath as one of the Cougars leaped above the other players and grabbed hold of the ball first as time expired. Everyone groaned in defeat, knowing the comeback had fallen just short. Everyone, that is, except Tristan. He was too busy pumping his fist in the air as his teammate raced across the goal line with the real football clutched in his hands.

The Cosmo player, who had made what everyone believed to be the game-ending catch, stared down in confusion at the object in his hands. What he thought was the ball turned out to be a leg with a gold lighting bolt painted on the side.

Just before the kickoff, Tristan had loosened the strap beneath his knee, and when his prosthetic had sailed past the necessary yardage, fooling almost everyone on the field, so had the ball—which Michael caught and ran in for the game-winning touchdown.

A deafening roar filled the night air as the Bay Herriman Bombers hoisted Tristan above their heads and the throngs of fans chanted his name. It was a comeback win for the ages, and even the Cougars couldn't help but applaud Tristan's heroic victory.

After the celebration ended and the stands began to empty, Tristan stood on the field as a man in a plaid sports jacket approached.

"Impressive moves out there," the man said. "I've never seen a game like that in all my years of covering this sport. You were the secret weapon. Why haven't I seen you on the field before?"

Tristan shrugged and refastened his prosthesis to his knee. "I don't get to play that much."

"You've got a good coach, but he'd be a fool if he didn't start you at quarterback next season."

Tristan smiled. "You think so?"

The man pulled something from his shirt pocket and handed it to Tristan. "See you around, Tristan Chidester. I'm sure we'll be in touch."

As the man walked away, Tristan looked down at the business card in his fingers.

Chip Chabot—Regional Scout for the San Francisco 49ers

FRANK L. COLE

Frank L. Cole was born into a family of Southern storytellers and wrote his first book at age eight. Sadly, he misplaced the manuscript and has since forgotten what he wrote. Highly superstitious and gullible to a fault, Frank will believe in any creepy story you tell him, especially ones involving ghosts and Bigfoot. Currently, along with his wife and three children, he resides in the shadows of a majestic western mountain range, which is most likely haunted. Frank has published seven books. His eighth, *The Afterlife Academy,* releases September 2015.

http://frankcolewrites.com/

TRISTAN

"All our dreams can come true, if we have the
courage to pursue them." —Walt Disney

Sada
(JPA Brain Tumor)

Meet Sada! At the request of Sada, and with some help from her mother, there is a bit more "Arrrgh" to her bio!

Ahoy! Meet me matey, Cap'n Sada. Sada has been battling juvenile pylocytic astrocytoma (a tenacious, bilge-rat-type of brain tumor) for over six years. It has been a long, hard battle that has caused her, her six siblings, and her parents to batten down the hatches more than once. This lass has had two brain surgeries since she was nine years old to remove five tumors, with the very real possibility of more surgeries to remove new ones that keep growing.

Aside from physical therapy and cancer treatments, the scallywag high pressure in her skull caused her to lose all vision in one eye and partial vision in the other. But she won't be walkin' the plank anytime soon since the rougher the seas, the smoother she sails. None of these scourges has taken away her strong spirit and awesome personality.

A common theme among these kids as they battle cancer is the idea of being free. Free from the hospital, free from the debilitating effects of cancer, free from treatment and the side effects—free to just be kids, savvy? For

 Sada, I think that being a pirate is the ultimate symbol of freedom.

147

SADA OF THE HIGH SEAS
Bobbie Pyron

SARAH SAT ON THE WINDOW SEAT IN HER BEDROOM gazing at a moon full and rich as a gold coin. "A pirate's moon," she sighed.

She knew this particular moon was called a Pirate's Moon because Sarah Bloomington knew everything there was to know about pirates. While most fourteen-year-old girls from respectable families were busy learning how to sew tiny, perfect stitches, she was busy learning to tie perfect knots—knots necessary to live aboard a ship—and sword fighting with imaginary opponents. While respectable girls read respectable books like *Jane Eyre* and *Little Women,* Sarah devoured *Treasure Island, The Three Musketeers,* and most especially, *The Pirate's Own Book*—books from her brothers, who had no interest in reading.

Sarah Bloomington had no interest in high society or being respectable. More than anything, she wanted to be a pirate, sailing the high seas seeking treasure and adventure.

"Please, please," she whispered to the moon, "help me."

The next day, Sarah's governess said, "We need to go into the village to pick up your debutante gown."

Sarah groaned. "But I don't *want* to debut! It's stupid! And I certainly don't want a gown."

The governess frowned. "All well-born girls debut. How else can the other families see what a good match you would make for their sons?" She smoothed down the girl's tangled hair. "Honestly," she said, "it's time for you to stop running around like a wild thing and become a proper lady."

The seaside village of Stormhaven bustled with activity. The smell of salt and fish and spices brought from faraway lands lifted Sarah's spirits. The salty sea breeze on her cheeks filled her with a bit of hope.

"I'm going down to the merchant stalls to buy something pretty for Mother," the girl lied.

Her governess frowned—again. "Don't go wandering down to the docks. It's no place for a girl." She squinted at the clock tower. "Meet me at Madame Chemise's in half an hour."

Of course, Sarah raced straight to the docks.

Her heart soared as she gazed up and up at the ships' tall masts, the white sails shining in the sun like gulls' wings. How she longed to climb to the crow's nest, holding a spyglass to her eye in search of ships to plunder or nameless islands to explore. How she longed to shed the confines of lace and corsets, shoes and stockings for the freedom of pants and bare feet. She would rather carry a sword than a parasol!

Sarah slowly made her way up the long steps to the village, leaving the docks behind. "I'll never be a pirate," she muttered. "I'll have go to a stupid ball in a stupid gown where everyone will look at me like a sheep at auction."

Just then a hearty gust of wind blew from the sea. A stained piece of paper swirled up from the docks, sticking fast against her leg.

As Sarah pried the paper from her leg, something caught her eye. The something was these two words: PIRATES WANTED!

Sarah gasped and read.

Pirates wanted! Captain seeking crew for upcoming voyage to faraway lands in search of buried treasure and other likewise riches. Scallywags, rapscallions, ruffians, and swashbucklers welcome. Respectable people need not apply. If interested in a life on the high seas, come to the Sea Wolf, *anchored in Lamb Harbor.*

Sarah could barely believe her eyes. A real pirate captain advertising for a crew! She read the flyer over several times, then frowned. "But when?" she asked the grease-stained piece of paper. "You don't say *when* I should apply." She turned the paper over, and there, scribbled in atrocious script, were the words, *We set sail on the morn of the 5th.*

Sarah frantically searched her mind for the date. Was today the fourth? Had the fifth already come and gone?

She tucked the advertisement into her sleeve and raced to the dress shop.

Her governess stood outside, glaring pointedly at the clock tower.

Sarah skidded to a stop. "I'm sorry I'm late, Miss Bunderbluss, but please, can you tell me what today's date is?"

The governess narrowed her eyes, ignoring the girl's question. "And where is the 'something pretty' you were going to get for your mother?"

Sarah grabbed the woman's arm and said, "*Please,* Miss Bunderbluss, what is today's date?"

The governess herded her charge toward the waiting carriage. "If you paid attention to normal things like other girls your age, you'd know." She handed the package containing the gown to the footman. "Today is June the fourth."

That night, Sarah feigned illness and retired to her room early. She paced back and forth, reading the advertisement over and over. "They set sail tomorrow morning," she muttered. "And if I know pirates—which I do—they'll sail at sunrise." It all seemed rather hopeless . . .

"No!" she said, striding to her wardrobe and flinging open the doors. "A pirate does *not* give up!" She looked through her clothes, and her heart sank. Nothing suitable for a pirate interview.

Then she remembered: her middle brother was away for the night. She crept down to his room and pilfered a pair of pants, two rough shirts, and, at the last minute, a canvas pack. "Sorry, Jack," she said with a smile. "I'll pay you back when I find the buried treasure."

Sarah changed into her brother's clothes and stuffed the canvas pack with underwear (she assumed even pirate's needed clean underwear), her toothbrush and paste, and, lastly, her love-worn copies of *Treasure Island* and *The Pirate's Own Book*. She would *not* take her parasol or her shoes.

With one last look at her room, she opened the window and slipped out into the night, the full moon showing her the way. On her pillow, she left a note that read, "Even girls need adventure!"

The chirping of birds woke the girl curled beneath a rock outcrop. She blinked against the bright sunlight and rolled over.

"Oh, no!" she cried, jumping to her feet. "I've overslept! They'll have sailed without me!"

She scanned Lamb Harbor but there, rocking gently on the waves, was the *Sea Wolf*. A flag with a smiling skull fluttered on the high mast in the breeze.

Sarah threw the canvas pack onto her back and raced down the path to the shore. No one stirred on deck.

Sarah cupped her hands around her mouth. "Ahoy, mateys! Ahoy, the ship!"

Nothing. Sarah frowned. "Where is everybody?"

She took a deep breath, cupped her hands around her mouth again, and shouted, "Hello! Hello!"

Nothing. Perhaps they were raiding the village or something equally piratey, and because she had overslept, she didn't get to go. Sarah picked up a rock from the sand and threw it at the side of the boat. *Whack!*

A man stumbled up from belowdecks, scratching his rather fat belly and squinting in the sun. "Here now, what's all the ruckus about?"

She stood as straight and tall as she could. "I've come to apply for work on your boat."

The pirate frowned. "You've come to sell us a goat?" He scratched his head. "Well, now, as it happens, er . . . You see . . ."

A pale, skinny pirate joined the first one. "How's a man supposed to get any sleep around here with all this shoutin' going on?"

Sleep? Sarah started to point out it was long past time proper pirates should be sleeping, but she thought better of it.

"No, no," the girl called, louder. "Your *boat*! I want to work on your *boat*!" She pulled the advertisement from her pocket and waved it.

"Oy," the skinny pirate said. "He says he wants to work on your boat, Captain."

The captain grinned. "Well, that's a different kettle of fish! Come aboard, boy!"

Sarah held the pack above her head and waded out to the *Sea Wolf*. Effortlessly, she climbed the rope ladder and hoisted herself over the rail.

"That was certainly some fine climbing, boy, I'll have to say," the captain said appreciatively.

"Wait just a blasted second," the pale pirate said, narrowing his eyes at Sarah. "You're no boy—you're a *girl*!"

Two unlikely-looking pirates joined the group. One peered at her through cracked spectacles. "I don't know about that, Casper, it could be a boy."

A pirate with unusually prominent ears peered around Casper. "I think it is a girl." His ears turned an alarming shade of red.

Sarah sighed impatiently. "Of course, I'm a girl. I've come to apply for work on the *Sea Wolf*." She studied the motley crew. "This *is* a pirate ship, is it not?" she asked doubtfully.

"Of course," Casper said, "but girls aren't allowed on a pirate ship."

Sarah frowned. "It doesn't say on your flyer that girls can't apply."

"Does too." Casper snatched the paper from Sarah's hand and pointed to the bottom of the page. "Right here: Respectable *people* need not apply."

"So?"

"So," Casper said. "Girls aren't 'people.'"

"Are too!" Sarah spat.

"Are *not*!"

Sarah threw her pack to the deck and roundly kicked Casper in the shins.

"Ow! Ow! Ow!" He hopped on one leg, clutching the other. "What did you go and do that for?"

The big-eared pirate hid behind the captain.

"See here," the captain said. "There's no need to fight."

Sarah's mouth dropped open. "No need to fight? But that's what pirates do! What kind of pirate ship is this?"

For the first time since coming aboard, Sarah took a good look around. No cannons. No swords or guns or treasure chests. The mainsail mast had no crow's nest, and the flag looked entirely too friendly.

She put her hands on her hips. "Why don't you have a crow's nest?"

"We're afraid of heights," the captain said.

"And there are no weapons of any sort," she pointed out. "How do you expect to raid villages or capture a merchant ship or fight off the royal navy?"

The hapless pirates looked from one to the other. "We're hoping a nice chat will do," the bespectacled pirate said, cleaning them with a monogrammed hanky.

"And a cup of tea," Big Ears added from behind the captain.

Sarah stared at the so-called pirates in disbelief. "My one chance to be a pirate and sail the high seas, find buried treasure, and have adventures, and I end up with . . . with *you* lot."

The girl sank to the deck and put her head in her hands.

"But don't you see?" the captain asked, touching her back. "That's what we want too."

Sarah looked up into the faces of the men. "Really?"

Casper nodded. "We just don't rightly know how."

Sarah took her worn copies of *The Pirate's Own Book* and *Treasure Island* from her pack and held them up.

"Are you willing to learn?" she asked. "Are you willing to work hard and stick together no matter what?"

They nodded eagerly.

She eyed Casper. "Even though I am a girl?"

Rubbing his shin, Casper nodded.

Sarah sprang to her feet, grinning. "I think this calls for a blood oath." She took a switchblade stolen from her oldest brother. She flicked open the blade and made a quick, sure cut across her finger. Blood dripped onto the deck. Big Ears fainted dead away.

Sarah rolled her eyes and shook her head. "I can see I have my work cut out turning you into proper pirates."

"But you can, can't you, miss?"

Sarah looked at the hopeful faces and the tight ship and the sun dancing like jewels on the endless sea beyond.

She laughed. "Hoist the mainsail and pull the anchor!"

"Captain," she ordered, "set a course south by southwest. We're headed for Jamaica!"

"Aye, aye, um . . . What should we call you, miss?" the captain asked.

Sarah paused. Somehow her name didn't sound like a pirate's name. Then she remembered what her littlest brother had called her when he was but three.

With a whoop, she leaped onto the quarterdeck. "Sada! Sada of the High Seas!"

BOBBIE PYRON

Bobbie was born in Hollywood, Florida, and grew up loving the ocean. Perhaps that is why she always wanted to be a mermaid. Or a frog. But she also wanted to be a writer.

Her life held many twists and turns: She went to college and earned degrees in psychology and anthropology. For a time, she was a singer in a rock-and-roll band. She returned to college for a degree to work as a librarian, a career she has enjoyed for over twenty-five years. Finally, she realized her dream and became a published author. She is the author of four books.

http://www.bobbiepyron.com

JORDAN

"The future belongs to those who believe in the beauty of their dreams." —Eleanor Roosevelt

BRAELYN
(Acute Lymphoblastic Leukemia)

MEET BRAELYN! The first time I met Braelyn I asked her who her favorite superhero was. With a big grin she immediately replied, "My mommy!" With tears in her eyes, Braelyn's mom was speechless; to her, Braelyn is the real superhero.

Braelyn wanted to be a superhero who saved her friends—her friends being her stuffed animals! I made the mistake of tying her animals to the tracks and that caused a bit of sadness, which almost ruined the shoot. Luckily we were able to explain that she would be saving her friends, which made her pretty happy!

On September 16, 2013, Braelyn was diagnosed with acute lymphoblastic leukemia, the most common form of childhood cancer. At three years old, Braelyn has already faced down her disease with superhero courage and strength. She doesn't seem to mope around the house feeling sorry for herself either. She is one of my personal heroes.

157

Braelyn and the Speeding Train

Peggy Eddleman

It was the sunniest of days when four-year-old Braelyn sat on a blanket in her yard, playing Plan the Party with her big sister, Dani. She gave all of her stuffed friends the most gigantic hug, and then sat them where they could watch. Braelyn's mom and dad were sitting in the sun, reading and chatting and ready to join in on whatever party their daughters planned. Braelyn and Dani had already planned some of the most exciting parties around—holiday parties and dance parties and board game parties and animal parties. Today's party needed to be extra special, though, to celebrate such a beautiful day.

Suddenly Braelyn turned and saw that her stuffed friends were gone! She had a terrible feeling deep in her chest that they were now far away and in big trouble. She jumped up and grabbed her cape, fastening it around her neck. "I'll be right back," she called out to her family. "I need to go save the day."

Braelyn grabbed her trusty scooter as her mom called out to her, "Good luck, sweetie!"

Her dad gave her two thumbs up. "Go be awesome, my little superhero!"

Her sister waved good-bye. "See you soon!"

Ka-chunk! Ka-chunk! Ka-chunk! Braelyn's scooter sounded as the wheels raced across the lines in the sidewalk. She pushed her foot on the ground faster and faster as she whizzed past all of the neighbor's houses. She was wearing her superfast shoes, and they were definitely making her go superfast. *Swish!* went the air as she flashed around the corner.

Everyone's heads whipped in Braelyn's direction as she passed through the neighborhood. She sped by so fast that she was barely a blur to them as she raced down the sidewalk.

When she got to where the street and the sidewalk ended and the fields started, Braelyn parked her scooter. Now that she was even closer to the danger, she could sense that she needed to save them fast!

Braelyn took off running. She ran across the field, her legs moving so fast that if it weren't for the *Thud! Thud! Thud!* her feet made as they hit the ground, she would have thought she was gliding across the fields.

When she reached the woods, she sped around each of the trees. She leaped over fallen logs and big rocks. She ducked under low tree branches. Left and right and over and under she went as she ran through the woods faster and faster. Everything around her became a blur of green and brown.

Finally! She made it past the very last tree and into the open. Train tracks ran alongside the woods as far as she could see in both directions. And standing right in front of the tracks was a very large bad guy.

His hair was as black as a spooky cave at nighttime, and it stuck out in all directions. Big bushy eyebrows scrunched down between his eyes, and his long skinny nose seemed to point right at Braelyn. His shoulders and stomach were so broad that she could barely see around him.

"You're too late to stop my plan," the bad guy said. Then he laughed an evil laugh that bounced off the mountains in the distance and echoed back.

He stepped to the side so Braelyn could see what he had been hiding. Her stuffed friends were tied up on the train tracks! She glanced to the right and saw a train barreling its way down the tracks in their direction. It would reach them at any moment! She needed to save them quickly.

No matter which way she moved to get to her stuffed friends, though, the bad guy stepped the same direction and blocked her. His arms were spread out wide, ready to stop her if she got close. Left and right and left and right they both moved. She couldn't get around him, and she didn't know what she was going to do to save her stuffed friends in time.

The train rumbled like thunder as it got closer, and the *Wooooooo-wooooooo!* of the horn rang in Braelyn's ears as it warned them to move away from the tracks. She was so worried about her friends, though. If she couldn't find a way to get past the bad guy, there would be no way to save them.

She *had* to find a way.

Braelyn stopped trying to get past the man and looked around. There was nothing nearby to help her—nothing but rocks and dirt and train tracks and weeds and trees. Then, out of the corner of her eye, she noticed that the bad guy had brought a lot of rope, but he hadn't used very much to tie up her stuffed friends. The rest lay looped in a circle on the ground at the edge of the woods.

She darted toward the rope, moving at her fastest superspeed, grabbed it, and raced back to the man. Around and around him she ran, twisting the rope as she went. Before the bad guy even realized what was happening, Braelyn had him tied up from his ankles all the way to his neck, his arms trapped close to his sides.

He tried to take a step toward her, but with his feet tied together, he fell back onto his rear. The man wiggled and wiggled, unable get free. He was trapped and couldn't stop her now.

But there was no time left! The train was almost to her friends, and they were in great danger. Braelyn ran toward them as the train's horn blared and the wheels rumbled and the big hulking train barreled closer, its shadow falling on Braelyn and her stuffed friends. With one motion she scooped her friends into one arm and threw her other arm toward the sky.

She leaped into the air, flying them up, up, up.

Just as Braelyn got them high enough, *Woosh!* went the air as the train sped past, barely missing them.

"That was close," Braelyn said to her stuffed friends as she glided to the ground as gently as a feather falling.

The train made a *clunk, clunk, clunk* sound as each car sped past in a blur, blocking the bad guy from Braelyn's view. The train roared down the tracks and out of sight, and when she could once again see him, Braelyn smiled a gigantic smile and did her Sassy Pants dance in triumph.

The bad guy tried to shake a fist at her, but couldn't while he was tied up. "You ruined my plans!" he shouted.

Warmth spread through Braelyn. "I saved my stuffed friends, and your days of evil plans are over!" She gave her stuffed friends a tight squeeze, then put her arm into the air and leaped into the sky.

This time she flew over the tops of the trees and across the fields, feeling the wind in her face as she flew. Up here, nothing held her down. She soared on the air, feeling it rush all around her.

A little bluebird changed its course and flew right next to her, chirping a happy chirp that sounded a lot like "Good job, good job" before flying away. Braelyn was so high in the air that all of the trees and houses and cars and people below her in the distance looked like little toys.

When she reached the place where the fields ended and the sidewalk began, Braelyn glided to the ground, making sure to give her stuffed friends a soft landing.

With her feet once again touching the ground, she tucked her stuffed friends tightly into her belt and grabbed hold of the handles on her scooter. She turned on her superspeed and pushed her foot on the sidewalk as fast as she could, making the scooter rocket forward.

In no time at all, she was steering her scooter back into its parking spot on her driveway. "Thanks for getting us home so fast, Trusty Scooter," Braelyn said as she patted the handles.

She carried her stuffed friends into the house and tucked them safely into bed. After such an adventure, they must be exhausted!

When she shared with her family the story of everything that had happened, her mom called the police and told them where to pick up the bad guy. Then her dad, her mom, and her big sister all wrapped her into a hug as big as the sky and as tight as a warm blanket.

Her dad kissed her on top of the head and said, "You saved the day, my little superhero."

Braelyn looked at her sleeping stuffed friends and smiled. She *had* saved the day.

PEGGY EDDLEMAN

Peggy Eddleman is the author of *Sky Jumpers* (a Bluebonnet Nominee, a Beehive Nominee, a Golden Sower Nominee, a South Carolina Book Award Nominee, an American Booksellers Association's ABC Best Book of 2013, a NYPL's 100 Books for Reading and Sharing selection, and a Kids Indies Next selection) and its sequel, *The Forbidden Flats*. Peggy lives at the foot of the Rocky Mountains in Utah with her husband and their three kids, who are all busy creating their own adventure stories.

http://peggyeddleman.com/

BRAELYN

"A hero is an ordinary individual who finds the strength to persevere and endure in spite of overwhelming obstacles." —Christopher Reeve

BREANN

(Osteosarcoma)

MEET BRE! When Bre was fourteen, she was diagnosed with osteosarcoma, a rare form of bone cancer. Her tumor was in her tibia, below her right knee. Before cancer, Bre was a talented dancer and typical teenager. After the doctors removed the tumor, Bre and her family were faced with a serious decision. Either amputate her right leg below the knee or attempt an experimental procedure to save the leg. They chose to try to save the leg!

Bre was told that with this experimental procedure it would take her two years to walk and she would likely never run or dance again. Within a year of the surgery, Bre was walking like a champ! She now walks without any help at all and is working on being able to dance again. This image is meant to inspire her and give her the strength to keep working toward her goals. Scan the QR code below to see how we created Bre's image.

THE DROP-OFF
Ally Condie

"THE WORST PART OF EVERY DANCE," ANNA'S FRIEND Tani tells her as they're out shopping for dresses together, "is the drop-off. Even if you've had the best date, you're like, *Do we kiss? Hug?* And then if one of you moves in and the other one moves back . . . awkward."

They're going to the Sweethearts Dance, which is girls' choice, so at least they got to choose their dates. Anna's picked wisely. She's chosen someone hot and nice and *interesting*. Because Anna does not like to be bored. She has no time for that.

Some people think it's because of the cancer that Anna doesn't like being bored. They think it's because she has a clock ticking away in her mind now, like her life is borrowed time or stolen time or special time. But the truth is, Anna has always been like this. Cancer didn't change her, not in that way.

Anna has *never* liked to waste time.

When she was little, she liked the movie *Finding Nemo.* Her favorite part was always when Nemo finally went to the drop-off, that part in the ocean where safety gave way to the unknown and the real adventure began. That's how she likes to live her life—like it's an adventure.

"Maybe the way to handle it is to tell him what you want when you're walking to the door," Anna says to Tani. "I'll just say, 'We're going to kiss when we get to the top of the steps,' and then we'll both know what to expect."

Tani shrieks with laughter. She looks at the dress Anna's wearing. "You look hot."

"I know," Anna says. She does. "So do you."

Tani grins.

The mirrors make dozens of Annas. A bunch of Tanis.

Anna's dress is short and sleeveless and black. The top has little gold embellishments, and the skirt is lace. The dress looks kind of like a figure skater and a rock star got together and designed it.

It is a great dress.

She's not wearing tights or nylons. She's used to both; she wore them for years when she was on her dance team, before the surgery. A few weeks ago she threw them all away, all the fleshy-colored ones and the sparkly ones, and it looked like a bunch of snakes had shed their skin in the trash.

"Oh, Anna," her mom said when she saw them in the garbage. "Those were still in great condition. And you know how much they cost."

"Nope," Anna had said. "I'm not giving my skin to someone else."

Although she probably actually would give her real skin to someone else if they needed it really badly.

She gave it to herself, after all.

That was where she'd felt the pain first, after the surgery. She had three options with her kind of bone cancer—osteosarcoma.

Rotationplasty. That meant having part of her leg removed while the part below the involved point was rotated and reattached. She'd need part of a fake leg, but she'd still have her own knee.

Amputation. Leg gone.

Limb salvage. The diseased part of her bone would be taken out and replaced with metal rods.

All of the options meant she would never dance again. Not competitively. Not with huge leaps and bounds and motion, motion, motion, the way she used to dance. She had dreams of being on television, choreographing for the stars. Crowds loved her. She lit them up. It wasn't just that she was good, although she was. So, so good. It was also that she brought them in, made them notice her.

Look at me, she used to think. *Look at me dance.* And they always did.

She chose limb salvage.

That meant they'd had to take skin from her hip. And that's where she'd felt the pain first when she woke up. Not in the rest of her leg, which had had its insides removed, the bones replaced, the skin sewn, every gutting and hard thing you could think of done to it. No, it was her hip, where they'd pulled away the skin to help out her leg.

Whiner, she said to her hip. *It's my leg that really has it bad. You suck. Shut up.* That cracked her up a little. But not much. The pain that first month went on and on. *This will end,* she told herself, *because it has to.*

And it did. They'd said it would take her two years to learn to walk again.

It took eight months.

She's proud of that.

Her scar is purple, wavy, impossible to hide even if she wanted to. She doesn't. What's to hide?

She has great legs even with the surgery scars.

Her legs are where her date, Cole's, eyes go. Not first. First his eyes go to her eyes, which makes her happy, and then he looks down at her legs and she knows he's checking them out, even though he's seen them before. He's seen the scar before, too.

"Wow," he says. "You look great."

Anna's dad raises his eyebrows. He's huge and strong as steel and scares every guy who likes Anna, but he's a mushy teddy bear where she's concerned. When they first found out about Anna's cancer, he couldn't talk about it without crying.

"Be back by midnight," he says to her.

"One," she says.

"Twelve-thirty," her mom says, "and you're welcome for that."

Her mom is not mush. Her mom is also steel like her dad, just at different times and in different ways. They take turns.

In the hospital, Anna hated the food, and so her mom became Anna's personal delivery person. Her mom got salads from Café Rio and breadsticks from The Pizza Factory and peppermint shakes from JCW's and anything else Anna wanted. Only certain things, the exact right thing. Anna would close her eyes and think about it. *What is the only thing in the world that sounds good to me right now?* And then it would pop up in her mind, and she'd tell her mom what she absolutely *had* to have to eat that day.

"This reminds me when I was pregnant with you," Anna's mom said. "I could only eat certain things or I'd throw up."

"A turkey sub from Jimmy John's is what I need today," Anna said. "With avocado."

"I think you were easier when you were inside of me instead of outside," her mom said, rolling her eyes, but she went and got the food anyway.

"I'll be back by twelve-thirty," Anna says now. She gives her parents each a hug and tries to get out of the house, but there's no escaping taking a few more pictures before she and Cole are finally on their way.

"What are you laughing about?" Cole asks her after dinner as they drive to the dance. Their group went to a McDonald's wearing their best outfits because for Sweethearts the girls are supposed to pay, and she doesn't have a ton of money. Neither do her friends.

Plus, it was great to watch the other customers' faces when they came in, dressed to the nines.

"Nemo," she says. "From the movie. What if you ate him tonight?"

Cole had ordered a fish sandwich, which was a gutsy move on a date. So far his breath smelled fine. He had gum.

"I probably did," Cole says, and that cracks her up.

"Have you seen the movie?" she asks.

"Oh, yeah," he says. Then he surprises her because he does an impression of the little squid who gets scared and does the squid equivalent of peeing its pants: *"You made me ink!"* His voice goes high and squeaky, so different from how deep it usually is.

And then she's laughing so hard she can't stop.

"Maybe they'll make another movie someday," he says, his voice back to normal.

"Yeah," she says. "*Eating Nemo.*"

This makes *him* crack up.

This is it, she thinks for a second as they walk inside the decorated school gym. *I'm at a dance. I'm alive.*

And she can still dance. Two years haven't passed yet—she's not even supposed to be walking according to the doctors—but here she is, slow dancing just fine.

Cole dances close, but not gross-close. Just good close. She can feel the muscles in his back move and she likes it. He smells good. He makes her laugh. Above the two of them the ceiling sparkles, it's dark, and the student council has strung up lights that look like stars. Sort of. Good enough.

People asked her after her surgery, "So what's your dream now? Now that you can't dance?"

They don't seem to get that *life* is her dream now. All of it. The big stuff. The little stuff.

Great dress. Glittering lights. Snow coming down outside. Cute boy laughing with her. Heart pounding, laughter in the car, friends waving at her from across the dance floor.

Look at me, she thinks, the way she used to when she danced in front of a crowd. But now she thinks, *Look at the way I live. This is my dream now. All of this. And everything to come.*

The night has been perfect, and she and Cole walk to the door together. He holds her hand because the snow is a little slippery underfoot but not bad.

So, she thinks, *this is the drop-off.* The night is cold and full of stars. Her dress feels light, swishes around her when she walks. When she breathes in, she smells cologne and snow and mint.

It turns out that she doesn't tell him they're going to kiss at the top of the steps.

But somehow, he knows.

ALLY CONDIE

Ally Condie is the author of the *New York Times* best-seller *Atlantia* and of the Matched trilogy, a #1 *New York Times* and international best-seller. *Matched* was chosen as one of YALSA's 2011 Teens' Top Ten and named as one of Publisher's Weekly's Best Children's Books of 2010. The sequels, *Crossed* and *Reached,* were also critically acclaimed and received starred reviews, and all three books are available in more than thirty languages.

A former English teacher, Ally lives with her husband and four children in Utah. She loves reading, writing, running, and listening to her husband play guitar.

http://allycondie.com/

WILLIAM
(Acute Lymphoblastic Leukemia)

MEET WILLIAM! I first met William at Primary Children's Hospital in Salt Lake City, Utah. This was his second bout with cancer, and things were progressing as normal—well, as normal as things can be when fighting cancer—and William was in pretty good spirits despite having being confined to a tiny hospital room for two weeks.

That day we discussed William's dream of becoming a dragon rider. I knew I wanted to do something really fun for him during our shoot.

We traveled to a secluded office building a couple miles up Big Cottonwood Canyon. The plan was to explore the woods and hills near the building. We were going to search for William's dragon! William and I had a great adventure searching for dragon hideouts. It was the first time I was able to see William just being a boy, full of life and adventure! And, as luck would have it, William was able to find a dragon.

WILLIAM AND THE DRAGON

J. Scott Savage

WILLIAM STARED AT THE SIDE OF THE MOUNTAIN as three of the city's most skilled knights stumbled from the entrance of a large cave and through the yellow mist that floated outside the dark opening like an evil cloud. The men's armor—normally the bright gold and red of the city's colors—was covered in black soot. One of the knight's swords had been melted into a shape like a large letter J. Coughing and gasping for breath, the men pulled off their helmets and revealed faces red from exhaustion . . . and fire.

"Report," commanded the king, who sat astride a great white stallion. The horse glanced toward the cave and whinnied, trying to trot away, but the king held the reins tightly. "Did you kill the beast?"

"No," said the largest of the knights, shaking back his sweaty blond hair. "The creature was too powerful to be defeated by a dozen men. Or three dozen, for that matter."

"It could eat a horse in one bite," said the knight beside him, a woman with long black hair that looked even darker covered by soot. She held out her bow, which was now little more than a blackened stick. "My arrows bounced straight off the monster's scaly hide."

William, the youngest son of the king, was only six. But even he could see the look of worry that crossed his father's face. In the two months since Nogard, the great red dragon, had taken up residence in a cave outside the city, over a dozen villages had been burned and hundreds of sheep had gone missing.

The knight with the blond hair was Barton, William's oldest brother, and the woman was his aunt. They were two of the fiercest warriors in the land. If *they* couldn't defeat the dragon, who could?

The king pushed back his crown and shook his head. "Is it possible we can negotiate with the beast? What does it want? Gold? Treasure? Land? I'll grant it anything to save my people."

The third knight, an old man with gray hair and a white beard that disappeared down the front of his neck into his armor, shook his head. "I am afraid not, Your Majesty. We tried offering the dragon whatever it wanted, but it can't be bought. I'm afraid the only way to stop Nogard is to defeat him."

Crag had been the king's advisor for more than thirty years. He was the wisest man William had ever met. If even he was discouraged, they were in deep trouble.

William's father sighed. "I'm afraid we have no choice, then. As long as the dragon is here, no one is safe. Since my best warriors could not kill it, my decision is made. We must leave the kingdom."

"No!" William cried. Leave their homes and lands? The castle had been in his family for hundreds of years. How could they desert it? And what about the farmers working their fields? If they left now, they'd have no money, no food. They'd starve this winter. "There has to be something we can do."

Barton examined his bent sword and let it fall to the ground. Sadly, the three knights mounted their horses, and the group began riding back toward the castle. William urged his little pony up to Crag's much larger horse. He leaned toward the old man. "Isn't there anyone who can stop the dragon?"

Crag gazed down at William with eyes so light blue they looked almost silver. "Perhaps someone with extreme courage could find a way." He raised a bushy white eyebrow. "Sometimes the bravest are not the biggest or the strongest."

William dropped behind the rest of the riders, deep in thought. *Someone with courage.* His father was brave. He was king of all the land. But he was leaving. His mother was brave. As queen, she ran most of the kingdom and held the townspeople together through all kinds of trials. His older brothers and sisters were brave. But none of them had been able to stop the dragon.

Then a thought occurred to William. It was such an amazing thought that he stopped his pony in the middle of the road. What about himself? Was *he* brave? Although William was only six, he'd gone through some hard things in his life. People said he was brave for the way he handled the hard things, but William didn't feel especially brave. In fact, sometimes he felt so scared he started to cry.

But as scared as he'd been, he never gave up. He never quit. Did that make him courageous? Crag had said that sometimes the bravest weren't the biggest or the strongest. William was not as big as his father or as strong as his brothers, but maybe, just maybe, he could be brave. Biting the inside of his cheeks, trying not to let his hands shake on the reins, he turned his pony around and headed back to the cave.

He was nearly to the side of the mountain before anyone realized what he was doing. "Come back!" everyone shouted. But by then William was already tying his pony up to a small leafless tree.

"Wait here for me," he said, rubbing his pony's mane.

Taking a deep breath, he closed his eyes and stepped through the yellow mist into the cave.

The first thing William noticed when he stepped into the darkness were the two gold circles high above his head. It took him a moment to realize the circles were the eyes of the dragon. The sight of those two huge glowing eyes made William want to run. But even though he was frightened, he continued into the cave.

"What are you doing here?" snarled a deep voice.

As William's eyes adjusted to the darkness, he could make out a huge red head with sharp horns, long teeth, and a pointy beard. William squeezed his hands together and said, "I want you to leave the kingdom alone."

The powerful dragon burst into startled laughter. "Are you going to stop me?"

William swallowed. His mouth felt dry, and his nose stung from the smoke-filled air. "I don't know how, but I'll try."

"Try this!" the dragon shouted. Before William could move, Nogard lunged forward, opened his cavernous mouth, and closed his jaws around William.

William looked about, blinking. He couldn't see a thing. "Where am I?" he shouted. *"Am I, am I, am I?"* his voice echoed back at him.

"You are in my stomach," the dragon growled.

William wrinkled his nose at the foul smell. "Disgusting."

Realizing he had to escape before he was dissolved by the dragon's stomach acid, he reached into his pocket. He was hoping to find something to cut his way out—a knife, maybe—but the only thing his fingers touched was the sparrow's feather he'd picked up the day before.

It was small, just like him, but somehow it would have to do. Clasping the feather between his fingers, William reached up as high as he could and tickled the inside of the dragon's throat. Nogard coughed. William tickled the dragon's throat again. Nogard coughed harder. William tried one more time, and the dragon coughed so hard that it threw William up.

William landed a few feet away from the dragon. As he pushed himself to his feet, he realized he was covered in dragon saliva. "Yuck," he said. "This will never come out of my leather armor."

The dragon cocked his large red head. "I've never seen anyone survive being eaten by a dragon before. Perhaps you should run away while you can."

Although his knees were shaking and his stomach felt tied in knots, William shook his head.

Nogard waggled his beard. "Aren't you scared?"

"Terrified," William admitted. "But I'm not going away until you agree to leave the kingdom alone."

The dragon sighed. "I sort of liked you too." He opened his mouth and blew a stream of fire directly at William.

William pressed his eyes shut as heat engulfed him, sure he was about to be cooked into a small, charred William-kebab. But when he opened his eyes, he was still standing. He looked down at himself, examined his armor the best he could in the darkness, and ran a hand over his head. Not a single hair was singed.

It took him a moment to realize what must have happened. "It's the dragon spit," he said. "If it's strong enough to protect a dragon's stomach from fire, I guess it's strong enough to protect me, too."

Nogard stepped toward William, his great claws tearing divots in the stone floor of the cave. "What weapons did you bring to fight me with, little man?"

William shrugged. "I don't, uh, actually have any weapons."

The dragon chuckled and spread his great wings. "You came to stand against me unarmed?"

Feeling a little embarrassed, William said, "My mother says I'm too young to play with swords and spears."

The great red dragon leaned close until the boy could feel the creature's hot breath on his face. His nostrils flared as he sniffed at William. "I swallowed you and yet you chose not to run. I scorched you with fire and you stood your ground."

William shuffled his feet.

"I have traveled the world far and wide," Nogard said. "Many warriors have tried to fight me. Every one of them wore their strongest armor. They carried thick shields and sharp weapons. They all trembled and fled when they beheld my power. Yet you, a boy, come against me without a single weapon, wearing simple leather armor. How do you explain this?"

William wasn't sure how to answer. He rubbed his hands on his pants, hoping the dragon wouldn't notice how grossed out he was by the spit. "I guess I've learned that it's okay to be afraid. But being scared doesn't mean you give up."

The dragon bent his front legs and lowered his head until his chin rested on the ground. "I have searched every kingdom for someone as brave as you. You are truly a person of courage. Climb onto my back."

William could hardly believe what he was hearing. "You mean you aren't going to eat me?"

"I never really liked the taste of humans," the dragon said. "I much prefer sheep. And chocolate. I really like chocolate."

"Me too!" William said. Grabbing the dragon's scales, he climbed onto the creature's thick neck. His short legs dangled on either side as the dragon stood.

"Hang on," Nogard said. The dragon bent his legs, spread his wings, and suddenly they were rocketing out of the cave faster than a speeding arrow. Wind blew back William's hair and cooled his cheeks. Together the two of them blasted through the yellow cloud and into the sky. It was like being on the back of the biggest, coolest bird ever.

Down below, William's father, brother, and the others looked up in terror before seeing William on Nogard's back.

"It's okay!" William yelled down to them. "He's my friend." Throwing back his head, William let out a whoop, and together he and Nogard soared toward the sky. It was the greatest day of his life.

Now the only thing he had to worry about was how to convince his mother to let him keep a dragon at the castle.

J. SCOTT SAVAGE

J. Scott Savage is the author of the Farworld series and the Case File 13 series. He grew up in Northern California and now lives in northern Utah in a windy little valley of the Rocky Mountains. He has a wonderful wife who has somehow stuck with him for more than twenty years, four great kids, and a spastic border collie.

http://www.jscottsavage.com/

JP

(Acute Lymphoblastic Leukemia)

Meet JP! JP is quite possibly the most confident and energetic kid I have ever met. You'd have no idea how sick he really is because JP has been fighting cancer for the majority of his life with confidence and hope and doing so like a champion. I have no doubt he is going to do great things with his life. In fact, he already has!

Anything Can Be approached the Utah Jazz basketball team with the idea of making JP an official Jazz player for a day. We thought it would be cool to see if he could maybe even play with some of the players during a game. The Jazz loved the idea and went above and beyond to make it happen for young JP. His dream actually came true, and the results were awesome.

To see how JP made the most of this rare opportunity, check out the QR code below.

THE NEW GUY
Chad Morris

I GOT A NEW GUY," MR. CLAY, THE ASSISTANT coach, said as he approached the head coach courtside. The largest crowd of the tournament already sat in their seats, and more and more people were filing in.

"Great," Coach Hill answered, watching his team of seventeen-year-olds warm up in a college stadium, the largest venue they had played in. He was tall and bald and held a small whiteboard in one hand. His team of competitive league players had clawed and hustled their way to the national championship game, to the place where college and even NBA scouts came looking for up-and-coming talent.

Unfortunately, now that the Minn brothers had moved overseas, Josh Tempkin was sidelined with an ankle injury, and Jamal Taggart had been sick more often than not over the last three weeks, he desperately needed more players. "Where is he?"

Clay cleared his throat. "Well, the rules say that anyone who is younger than eighteen and hasn't played on any other team in the league this year is eligible." He spoke quickly, wringing his hands.

"Yeah," Coach Hill said.

"The kid I found is a little young, but he can play."

"As long as he can play," the coach said, jotting down a note at the top of his board.

"He's quick and accurate and always follows his shot," Clay said. "But looking at him, you wouldn't think—"

"Hopefully we won't need him," Coach Hill interrupted, glancing back at his assistant. "He's just backup for an emergency. Where is he?"

The assistant coach looked down. The coach's eyes followed much lower than he probably anticipated. Below Assistant Coach Clay's waist was a spikey-haired blond boy with a huge smile. He was wearing the Jaguars' green-and-gold uniform.

"You've got to be kidding," Coach said, shaking his head. "A five-year-old kid?"

"I'm six," the boy corrected.

"You'll be trampled."

"He'll be fine," Coach Clay defended. "He can—"

"Everyone else out there is seventeen. They are some of the best young players in the nation! I need someone who can keep up with them," Coach said, "not someone they need to babysit."

"He can keep up," Clay promised, his voice crisp. "JP's like a miracle. He had leukemia, but once he started to recover, he just never stopped. His body kept getting stronger and faster and—"

"We aren't interested in anyone his age," Coach interrupted.

"Just let him show—"

"No."

"If you'll just watch—"

"No." The coach's voice had grown louder, deeper. "I don't care how good he is. He's five."

"Six," JP corrected again, shifting the ball from one hand to the other, and then around his back. His movements were fluid.

"Cute," the coach said. "There's no way he's up to our level, and they"—he gestured toward his team warming up on the court—"would be humiliated to have him on the court." He turned to JP. "Sorry, kid, I won't even let you warm up with them.

And there is no way you're getting into the game. The best I can do is let you sit on the bench."

Thirty minutes later, Coach Hill vaulted off the bench to yell at the refs for the forty-somethingth time. The game had not gone well. The Tornadoes had jumped out to a quick lead, and the Jaguars had never come close to catching them. They were outmanned, outmuscled, and outplayed.

"Foul on number fifty-four, Jaguars," the ref yelled, pointing at the Jaguar center, a tall kid with dark skin and a buzz cut. Coach Hill palmed his forehead. The buzzer rang twice, and the overweight man at the table raised his full hand, signaling five fouls. Fifty-four was out of the game.

The coach looked down the bench. Two of his players had fouled out, his team was down eighteen points with eight minutes left, and if he didn't put someone in, they would forfeit the championship. "There are NBA scouts in the audience," he mumbled to himself. "I can't believe I'm doing this." He pointed at the six-year-old blond kid. "Boy. TJ."

"JP," the boy corrected.

"Whatever," Coach Hill said, waving off the mistake. "I'm putting you in."

JP leaped off the bench and tore away his athletic pants to reveal his bright green shorts.

"But," Coach said, "stay out of the way. I don't want you getting hurt."

JP's only answer was a broad smile.

As JP knelt by the scorer's table before entering the game, the assistant coach looked back at Coach Hill. "Don't worry." He clapped his hands. "This is going to be good."

"Don't worry?" Coach Hill blurted. "I just put a first-grader in the championship game. He's going to be steamrolled by kids three times his age. Half of them have shoes as tall as he is."

Coach Clay chuckled. "Your phone has a camera, right?"

"Yeah. So?"

"You might want to get it ready."

The man at the scorer's table sounded the buzzer, and JP entered the game. Murmurs and laughs ran through the crowd. The Jaguars hung their heads.

"Seriously?" the Tornado power forward asked. There was a hint of insult to his voice. And the refs argued JP was too young to play.

JP just kept smiling.

Coach Clay had to explain the official rules, and reluctantly everyone agreed JP could play. Soon the players lined up at the foul line for the Tornado player to take his shot. JP stood outside the three-point line, guarded by a boy twice his size. The player at the line dribbled twice, exhaled, and shot.

Swish.

He repeated the same ritual but missed the second attempt. JP took off down the floor, calling for the ball. The Jaguar who got the rebound launched it without thinking.

"What? Don't throw it to the kid," another Jaguar protested.

But JP jumped toward it. An audible gasp sounded from the crowd. The small boy with spikey blond hair hung several feet in the air. It was like his shoes were trampolines. With the grace of a gymnast, he clutched the ball and landed on the run. He raced farther down the court, dribbling without looking down. It was unbelievable. He could dribble like he breathed. He hit the key, took a few steps, and went up for a layup. Two points.

Silence.

The crowd and all the players on the court stood dumbfounded. The ref didn't even signal the basket good. The scorer's table didn't put the points on the board. Everyone was stunned, mouths open.

Coach Clay clapped, turning toward Coach Hill. "I tried to tell you."

It took a moment, but soon the refs shook their heads and got back to their jobs. The points went on the scoreboard.

The Tornado point guard brought the ball down and passed to the wing. But as soon as the player's back was turned, JP dashed in behind him and stole the ball. (It's tough to see a kid coming when he's half your size and faster than most small cheetahs.) JP bolted down the court, faked one way, and then passed it the other. He hit thirty-one on the run, who scored an easy floater.

The crowd began to clap.

Both teams went back and forth, scoring points, but thanks to JP's two more steals, five assists, a jumper at the top of the key, and a swished three-pointer, the Jaguars were within three points with only thirty seconds left.

They passed the ball to JP, who rocketed toward the hoop. Though his defender had much longer legs, he had a tough time keeping up with him. The center for the Tornadoes came up to help, but JP lobbed the ball. His teammate caught it and dunked it through the hoop in one swift motion.

Coach Hill took another picture on his cell phone. He had taken thirty-five in the last few minutes, each highlighting JP's abilities.

Coach Clay laughed and tilted his own cell phone screen to show JP playing outside at a park. It must have been where the assistant coach discovered him.

JP had led a comeback. The Jaguars only needed a defensive stop and one more basket to win.

Before the Tornado player passed in the ball, JP's teammate gave him a high five. "I don't know how ya do it, but I like it, kid."

JP's smile grew as he got ready for a full-court defensive press.

At first the Tornadoes seemed poised to break under the pressure, but one player rushed a pass, and the ball floated out of reach of his teammate and out of bounds.

Jaguars' ball. Eighteen seconds left.

JP dribbled at the top of the key until the clock counted down to eight, the crowd cheering and rising to its feet. Win or lose, the Jaguars wouldn't leave time for the Tornadoes to get the ball. In a flash, JP spun on the dribble, catching his defender on his heels. Players rotated, trying to catch JP or follow their man.

Then JP saw it—a weakness. One of the Tornado forwards didn't roll out with the player he was supposed to defend. JP bounced the ball, and another Jaguar caught it, turned, and shot. The crowd held its breath as the ball floated gracefully with a perfect backspin. JP would get his final assist, and the Jaguars would win the championship with only a second left.

But the ball rolled around the rim and popped out.

One second left.

The ball only made it about a foot away from the rim when an outstretched hand stopped it. It was a small hand. A six-year-old hand. It was the hand of JP Gibson, who had jumped over eight feet in the air. The smallest kid on the court was airborne with the ball, soaring over the hoop. He dunked it home just before the buzzer sounded. The glass on the backboard shattered as the ball blasted through the net. JP crashed to the floor, the rim still in his hand. Broken glass scattered across the hardwood around him.

The crowd erupted in cheers. Coach Hill bounced across the court. As he and Coach Clay ran to congratulate their team, he called, "I will never underestimate a six-year-old ever again."

JP rode his teammates' shoulders, and the crowd rushed the court. A man called out that he was an NBA scout and wanted to talk to JP, make him the youngest professional player in history. Two other scouts said something similar.

JP just smiled.

CHAD MORRIS

Chad Morris grew up wanting to become a professional basketball player or a rock star. After high school, he wrote and performed sketch comedy while going to college, and eventually he became a teacher and a curriculum writer. He is the author of the Cragbridge Hall trilogy. He lives in Utah with his wife and five kids.

http://chadmorrisauthor.com/

ETHAN
(Acute Lymphoblastic Leukemia)

MEET ETHAN! Ethan wanted to be a doctor as well as Batman. Seemed reasonable to me! One reason he wanted to be a doctor was because he was inspired by the good doctors who fought beside him throughout his battle with cancer.

I have found that so many kids who face this disease have a sense of empathy for the struggles of others. Ethan embodied, for me, so much of the good that comes from cancer. Good *can* and does come from hard struggles. We just have to be ready to recognize and appreciate those good things.

In October 2014, Ethan's family decided they wanted to celebrate all of the remaining holidays for the year in one week. With the help of some neighbors, friends, and an entire community, they were able to make this happen for Ethan. In one week they celebrated Halloween, Thanksgiving, Christmas, and New Year's. Ethan passed away shortly after that week of holidays.

Some might say that Ethan did not defeat his cancer, but I disagree. He beat his cancer by the way he lived and the example of courage he showed us all.

189

Batkid Versus the Bully
Brandon Mull

West Jordan, UT, a peaceful neighborhood, April 29, 3:37 p.m.

On a lonely suburban street, a glossy black sedan slows, engine quiet. The still neighborhood looks like it might have been evacuated, except for young Andrew Trent, following a pebble along the sidewalk, catching up to the stone only to send it skittering ahead with the toe of his tennis shoe.

Andrew fails to notice the sedan until it eases to a stop, tires grinding grit into the asphalt. A tinted window slides down with hardly a whisper, and the barrel of a plastic gun the size of a cannon extends from inside the plush car. Before Andrew can move, a red dodgeball launches from the mouth of the weapon with a low *whoomp* and whistles through the air.

The rubbery slap leaves Andrew's face hot and stinging. His backpack goes flying, and he strikes the ground before he knows what hit him. Head swimming, he sits up as the sedan accelerates on screaming tires.

Behind him, the dodgeball rolls to a stop on a neatly trimmed lawn.

West Jordan Regional Medical Center, April 29, 4:33 p.m.

Dr. Ethan VanLeuven sits at a small desk completing his charts, when his pager goes off. Not the black pager—the red one. It has been a long day, but he helped a lot of people. As usual, many of his patients were skeptical about him at first, due to his young age. But his loyal nurses had pointed out that somebody who completed medical school as a kid was probably smarter than somebody who finished their residency well into their twenties.

Sure, he has a little desk to fit his small stature. His scrubs are undersized as well. But any medical professionals who have worked with him agree that he is one of the best.

The red pager means a long shift is about to get longer. Ethan doesn't use the red pager for medical emergencies—it only sounds when somebody needs Batkid.

After checking to be sure nobody is approaching his office, Ethan rushes to the third filing cabinet from the left, inserts his key, and opens the entire front of the cabinet like a door. Ethan steps inside and descends into his med-lair. It doesn't feature as much gear and equipment as the sub-basements beneath his mansion, but it contains the essentials, including his mask and his body armor.

Sipping a fresh cup of hot chocolate, Ethan signs in to his computer. The images come up right away. The victim is a kid in this very hospital! The boy, Andrew Trent, has been admitted with a mild concussion. His face looks like somebody has played tetherball with it.

Zooming in on the image, Ethan notices patterned grooves on the boy's skin, telltale hints about the surface of the object that struck him. Forget the tetherball reference—this was done by a dodgeball. And not just any dodgeball. This one had traveled at an incredible velocity.

As far as Ethan knew, only one person in the state of Utah had the means and motivation to fire dodgeballs at that speed. People called him the Bully.

West Jordan Regional Medical Center, April 29, 9:45 p.m.

Andrew Trent lies in bed, staring at the shadowy ceiling of his hospital room. His mother slumps in a nearby chair, asleep, her magazine still open on her lap. A sudden draft catches his attention, and Andrew turns to see a figure silhouetted near the window, the nearby curtains rippling gently.

The figure closes the window and approaches the bed. Andrew's jaw drops. Even in the dim lighting, there is no mistaking the intruder's small stature, sleek armor, and masked features. It's Batkid!

"Hi, Andrew," Batkid says quietly.

"What are you doing here?" Andrew asks, surprised.

"You were the victim of an unusual crime," Batkid says. "I spent some time investigating the scene."

"Do you know who did it?" Andrew asks eagerly.

"I suspect a criminal known as the Bully," Batkid says. "He's been causing trouble over the last few weeks. But I still don't know his identity. Tell me what you saw."

"A black car," Andrew says. "By the time I looked over, a big gun was pointed at me. The ball hit me before I could react. Am I going to be all right?"

"You have a few symptoms of a mild concussion," Batkid says. "You're only here overnight as a precaution. I expect you'll feel back to normal by tomorrow. Did you see a face?"

"I was looking down the barrel of a gun," Andrew says. "All I saw was that yellow plastic tube pointed right at me. I thought it might shoot water or Nerf darts. Then the dodgeball hit me and I went down. By the time I got up, the car was out of sight."

"You're a fourth grader?" Batkid asks.

"Yeah."

"Fairly big for your age," Batkid observes.

"One of the biggest in my grade," Andrew replies.

"Do you get bullied much at school?"

Andrew snorts. "No."

Batkid nods thoughtfully. "Last week another kid from your school was found in a park with an atomic wedgie."

Andrew chuckles. "I heard about that."

"Some incredible force had pulled his underpants up over his head," Batkid says. "Poor kid. Tim Ross is his name. Not a little guy either."

"Tim's pretty big," Andrew agrees.

"Does he get bullied much?" Batkid asks.

"No way," Andrew says. "If anything, people watch out for him."

"I spoke with Tim after the incident," Batkid says. "The way he answered my questions left me with a hunch that he might pick on smaller kids sometimes."

"Good hunch," Andrew said. "I've seen him do it."

Batkid stares at Andrew. "Have you ever been the bully?"

Andrew looks away. "I'm tired."

"I need a straight answer," Batkid insists. "I have to solve this before somebody really gets hurt. If you don't want to talk, I can visit your school and ask around."

"Maybe sometimes," Andrew admits, still avoiding eye contact. "Kind of."

"None of the Bully's victims have been shrimpy kids. So my question becomes, who bullies the bullies?"

"The biggest bully," Andrew says. "Maybe that's how he shows off."

"Could be," Batkid says. "But does a bully usually mess with tough kids? Does he risk getting humiliated? Or does he go after the easy victims?"

"What if he's so tough that everybody is an easy victim?" Andrew asks.

"Possible," Batkid says. "But this bully uses ambushes and gadgets. Nobody has seen him. He may not be big. He may just be smart. Bullies make enemies. What if this is about vengeance?"

"You think I was attacked by somebody I bullied?" Andrew asks.

"It's worth investigating," Batkid says. "Could you give me a list?"

"Why not?" Andrew says. "Naming them might be a good way to check whether I have brain damage."

West Jordan, UT, a large house set back from the street, April 30, 2:13 a.m.

A cool breeze wafts across the yard, making a tire swing slowly rotate and sway. Batkid scans the area with his infrared spyglass but detects no heat signatures. Hopefully that means a dog won't spring out of hiding and attack.

He drops from the fence into the yard. All remains silent. The sizeable house is dark, but a dim light shines from the window above the unattached garage. Treading lightly, Batkid moves in that direction.

Having already visited the homes of three other kids on Andrew's list, Batkid has saved this house for last. The boy who lives here, Danny Welch, won the state science fair the last three years, each time with a mechanical marvel. Of all the kids on the list, he seems the most likely to have the skills to create dodgeball launchers and wedgie givers.

And of all the kids on the list, Batkid doesn't want Danny to be guilty. Ethan has entered and won science fairs as well. He builds his own gadgets. He likes smart, inventive people. Though it would mean a dead end for his investigation, a big part of him hopes he'll find no evidence here, just like at the other homes he's visited tonight.

After reaching the stand-alone garage, Batkid sneaks along the wall to a window. Peering through the glass, his night-vision goggles reveal a dark-colored sedan.

Batkid crouches down, mind whirling. There are many dark sedans in the world. This proves nothing. But he has samples from the asphalt where the Bully peeled out after shooting Andrew with the dodgeball. If those samples match the tires, he has found his man.

Rising, he cuts a small hole in a pane of glass, reaches in, unlocks the window, slides it up, and climbs into the garage. As his feet hit the ground, Batkid hears a wet *whoosh* and dives to one side. An enormous clump of soggy paper squishes against the wall beside the window, missing him by inches.

"Giant spitwad," Batkid murmurs. "Looks like I've found my guy."

Another *whoosh* sends a second spitwad his way. Batkid rolls to the side just in time, and the gooey mass of paper hits the floor with a juicy splat.

The second shot helps Batkid identify the source of the spitwads. His night-vision goggles reveal a cannon mounted to the ceiling. Aiming at the wires where the cannon is anchored, Batkid hurls a custom throwing star.

Sparks sizzle and the cannon goes slack.

Batkid races to the door at the rear of the garage. After kicking it open, he starts up the stairs, but a wind machine roars to life, blasting sand down the stairway and making his cape flap like a flag in a hurricane.

Sand in the eyes. Classic low blow. Grateful for the goggles protecting his vision, Batkid fights his way up the stairs and unplugs the wind machine.

Hurrying down the hall, Batkid reaches a door with light bleeding out the bottom and kicks it open. Beyond the doorway, a kid stands on his bed in red pajamas, holding a yellow plastic gun, ready to fire.

Batkid falls flat as the dodgeball is launched. The ball swishes over his head, rebounds off the wall, and returns straight at the kid who shot it. The boy gets nailed in the chest and spins off the bed, landing on the floor.

Batkid rushes over, places a boot on the kid's chest, and tears the dodgeball launcher from his grasp. The boy isn't very big. "Danny Welch," Batkid says.

"You're as good as they say," Danny replies.

"I have good days and bad, just like anybody else," Batkid says. "Today isn't your good day. You've been bullying people."

"I've teased the biggest jerks around," Danny says defiantly. "They all had it coming. I wasn't really hurting anybody."

"You sent one kid to the hospital," Batkid informs him. "He seems fine, but you could have caused him serious harm. You've been bullied. You don't like it. But becoming a bully yourself isn't the answer."

"So I just let them wail on me?" Danny asks. "I let them trip me and smash my dioramas and take my lunch money?"

"Some of the gear you're using could get you into major trouble with the law," Batkid says. "You don't want a criminal record."

Danny sighs and lowers his eyes. "No. But I don't like being bullied, either."

"You've already sent a clear message," Batkid says. "If you vow to stop using your talents for revenge, I'll talk to the kids who picked on you. I'll tell them the Bully is temporarily out of commission. But I'll warn them that he could be back."

"How is what I did different from what you do?" Danny asks.

"You were after revenge," Batkid says. "You traded violence for violence. I'm trying to uphold the law. I protect this city. Especially when somebody stronger preys on somebody weaker."

Danny chuckles softly. "There aren't many people weaker than me."

Batkid shakes his head. "Are you kidding? With the weapons you developed, you're one of the most powerful people in town. You need to harness those abilities for good. Trust me, Danny, revenge is beneath you."

"Okay," Danny says. "I'll quit. I promise. But this will leave me in need of a hobby. Would you like an assistant?"

"Tell you what," Batkid says. "You stay out of trouble for six months and then we'll talk."

"Fair enough," Danny says. "You're really not going to bring me in?"

"Not if you keep your word," Batkid says. "We misunderstood geniuses have to stick together."

"Thanks, Batkid," Danny says. "Sorry for the trouble I caused. I don't suppose there's any chance you'll tell me who you are under that mask?"

Ethan smiles. "That's a secret for another day."

BRANDON MULL

Brandon Mull is the author of the *New York Times, USA Today,* and *Wall Street Journal* best-selling Beyonders and Fablehaven series. His newest series, Five Kingdoms, is about a group of friends who get kidnapped into another world. Brandon resides in a happy little valley near the mouth of a canyon with his wife and four children. He spent two years living in the Atacama Desert of Northern Chile, where he learned Spanish and juggling. He once won a pudding-eating contest in the park behind his grandma's house, earning a gold medal.

http://brandonmull.com

Acknowledgments

Thank you to my amazing wife, Elizabeth Diaz, who has stood by me throughout this process from the beginning. She is always honest with me when it comes to my work and pushes me to do better. At the same time, she is my biggest fan and supporter, and I could not have done this without her. I lean on her for strength as I work to make my dream come true!

Thank you to all my family, Mom and Dad, mother- and father-in-law, and everyone else who has believed in me and made this a success.

Huge thanks to Amanda Flamm for helping me with this project from the beginning. Thank you for taking a chance on my crazy idea to make the dreams of cancer fighters come true. You and the wonderful people of Millie's Princess Foundation gave so much time to this project, and for that we will always be grateful.

Thanks to the ACB team and all of your hard work and dedication to this project: Elizabeth Diaz (Project Manager), Kristen Hackett (Operations Director), Lindsay Moore (Art Director), Andrea Terry (Social Media), Kristen Larsen (Dream Maker), and Cathy Krimme (Accountant).

Huge thanks to the following individuals for giving so much of their time to this project: Amanda Flamm, Brady Flamm, Lisa Teran, Ashley Alhquist, Elizabeth Flamm, Christine Bowman, Brett Bergener, Scott Windes, and Andres and MerriLyn Diaz.

This book would not be possible without the extremely talented authors who gave of their time and talents to make this book truly spectacular: Stephen R. Andrews, Frank L. Cole, Ally Condie, Kristyn Crow, Peggy Eddleman, Linda Gerber, Sharlee Glenn, Shannon Hale, Clint Johnson, Sara B. Larson, Brandon Mull, Chad Morris, Jennifer A. Nielsen, Lehua Parker, Bobbie Pyron, J. Scott Savage, Liesl Shurtliff, Adam Glendon Sidwell, Jess Smiley, Ilima Todd, and Tyler Whitesides.

A huge thank-you to our sponsors and donors: Millie's Princess Foundation, Operation Kids, Timm Hilty and the Silver Queen Art Gallery, Bergener and Associates, James Bergener, Lee Byram, Patti Hodson, Megan Nielsen, LaNeece Flamm, Nico Snow Tibbels, Karen Byers, Jennifer Preston, Frank Ball and Preston Tait, Michael Powell, Shawne and Ian Schorvitz, Ryan and Kristen Hackett, Robert and Carol Warren, George and Diane Bruschke, Kim Snider, Sabrina, Rache and Eric Schmidt, Kathlene Metcalf, Denise Garcia, Dan and Georgie Molinsky, Pam Kern, Hyland Cyclery, Mark Goodman, Cam Wood, Eddie Buckley, BNI Goldmine, Seven Times Seven, Persnickety Clothing Company, Thomas Arts, Dan Farr, Susan Cottrell, Sweet Tooth Fairy, Jylaire Thorell, FinFun, Skull Candy, Pat Carver, iFly Utah, Jon Bird and the Salt Lake City Dragons, Colton Satterfield, John Bethers, and Ramp Riot.

The following people gave a ton of time to make the images truly stand out:

For costumes, thank you to Rebecca McKinney, Lindsay Moore, Jeremy Bird, David Powell, Kyle Moore, and Erika Butler.

For hair and makeup, thank you to Jillian Joy, Danielle Donahue, Mary Cruz Horne, Suzanne Gallegos, Marci Briggs, and Valecia Sarmento.

For props, thank you to Denise Wagaman, Jesse Grabowski, Heather Donahue, and Christine Winn.

For video production, thank you to Holly Tuckett, Thomas Arts, Jade Teran, Nate Sorensen, and Tahlee Scarpitti.

For allowing us to use their wonderful locations, thank you to John and Amy Garff, Salt Lake City Comic Con, Dan Farr, Heidi Dunfield, Jon Briggs, Utah Jazz,

Gayle Miller, Greg Miller, Richard Smith, United Fire Authority Station 104, United Fire Authority fire training, Brian Anderton, Doug Hannay, Thayne Stembridge and family, Black Diamond Gym, Holly Brain, University of Utah football team, Jeff and Nancy Flamm, Creative Arts Academy of Utah, Craig and Bev Hackett, Rocky Mountain Raceway, Wasatch Indoor Bike Park, Rockin' D Ranch, Maritime Museum of San Diego, Ben Ehlert, Mitch Stevens, and Jonny Patterson and the Dreamathon.

Thank you to our models and photo assistants: Wasatch Renaissance Arts Foundation, University of Utah football team staff, Trevor Reilly, Jeremy Barton, Maddie Butler, William Taufoou, Jake Diaz, Tom Diaz, Ben Diaz, and Lucy Diaz.

For web and logo design, thank you to Cause Brands, Avant8, Ross McGarvey, and Brian Fogelberg.

For printing services, thank you to Nichols Photolab.

And finally, huge thanks to the Shadow Mountain team—Laurel Christensen, Chris Schoebinger, Lisa Mangum, Rachael Ward, Shauna Gibby, and Richard Erickson—for taking a chance on this book and making it such a wonderful experience.